Murder Is Bad Press

By: Alice Judge

Copyright © 2024

All Rights Reserved

ISBN: eBook: 978-1-961617-63-

ISBN: Paperback: 978-1-961617-8

ISBN: Hardcover: 978-1-961617-8

DEDICATION

To my husband Leo, who was my love and advocate. Gone but always in my heart.

ACKNOWLEDGMENT

Over the years there have been many people that have encouraged me in my writing. And, to them, I say "thank you." But there have been a few people that have prompted me to take my work out of the file drawer and put it out there for others to read. Toward that end I would be remiss if I didn't thank Steve Sherlock for his vast computer knowledge and patience tutoring me in that technology. Also, my daughter Heidi, for instructing me in that technology when I've forgotten all I once knew about it. Thank you also to my son Mike who, like his father, always read my writing and would call me to say how much he liked it. Thanks to Peter Fasciano, head of the local cable company for his forward thinking in bringing my writing group to the airways, permitting me to dust off my manuscripts and share my writings. Our writing group can be heard on Franklin radio, 102.9 FM weekends. This is a group of talented writers and the stories are wonderful. Tune in and you'll see.

Contents

Dedication i
Acknowledgment ii
About the Author.. v
Chapter 1 1
Chapter 2 10
Chapter 3 27
Chapter 4 32
Chapter 5 41
Chapter 6 47
Chapter 7 58
Chapter 8 63
Chapter 9 76
Chapter 10 82
Chapter 11 89
Chapter 12 102
Chapter 13 109
Chapter 14 118

Chapter 15 130

Chapter 16 133

Chapter 17 140

Chapter 18 151

Chapter 19 164

Chapter 20 170

Chapter 21 181

Chapter 22 189

Chapter 23 195

Chapter 24 203

Chapter 25 213

Chapter 26 226

Chapter 27 254

Chapter 28 264

Chapter 29 277

Chapter 30 281

Chapter 31 303

About the Author

This is Alice Judge's first book of a three-book series featuring Allison Peters, staff reporter, Sandy Ridge, Maine. But Alice has been a writer for many years. First as a newspaper correspondent and feature writer for two daily newspapers south of Boston, Massachusetts. Then, as a Creative Writing teacher for seventeen years in night school classes. Alice loves to write; be it inspirational stories or poetry, essays, and memoirs. Alice sees possible stories everywhere and has written many fictional short stories and novels. Those who know her writing have convinced Alice to share her fictional prowess with others, hence, MURDER IS BAD PRESS.

Chapter 1

I was talking to my sister Joan when I heard my newspaper editor, Bill Shaw, buzz me on my intercom. "Joan, the big man is paging me." I quickly rang off and made strides toward his office.

"The cops found a dead female in the woods at the corner of Wilson and Pickett. See what it's all about." I grabbed my purse and left with a heavy heart. Was the dead body my missing roommate, Blaire Nugent? I hadn't known her long, but I didn't wish her harm. Shaw had hired Blaire when she applied for a writing job. When I was introducing her to the newsroom, she mentioned she needed to find a place to live. I have an extra bedroom, which I offered her. I needed the extra money a renter would give me. Shaw sent Blaire out to cover a meeting that evening. My new roommate never came home, nor could anyone at the meeting tell me she had been there.

Wilson and Pickett Streets were way across town. Fortunately for me, I made all the green lights. All of Sandy Ridge's finest were at the site, plus a couple hundred onlookers. I slowly inched my way toward Police Chief Ed Hall.

"What is it, chief?"

"Some cute young thing that doesn't look cute anymore." Hall shook his head. "Someone wanted to make sure she was dead."

I thought of Blaire.

"Can I see the body?" Hall shot a look at me. "Easy does it, hot shot reporter. The medical examiner is with the body now. You don't get into the crime scene. You know that."

I stayed another hour, trying to piece overheard conversations together, then decided to look for the Medical Examiner, Dave Burger. I couldn't rest until I knew.

Burger didn't seem to be surprised to see me. "I knew I'd see you sometime tonight. I won't have anything conclusive on the girl for several days."

"Just tell me how old she was, and I'll leave you alone for a while. I promise."

"Allison, her face was badly bruised. And there was head trauma. She must have been hit from behind, tried to get up, and was hit again several times."

Someone in her twenties?" I asked, getting impatient.

Burger looked at me strangely. "Do you need to tell me something?"

I sat down, telling him I thought it might be my missing roommate. Burger said he didn't know I had a roommate. I told him about Blaire getting hired at The Courier and how I asked her to be my roommate. I told him about the meeting she was supposed to have covered and how Blaire hadn't come home. I told him how guilty I felt about not helping her. He listened intently.

"How old is Blaire?" he asked

"Two years younger than me. Twenty-four. " And her build?" asked Burger.

"Shapely." I thought back to how I saw the guys at The Courier practically salivate when looking at her. He smiled.

"Well, continue to look for Blaire, Allison."

I stared at Burger. He put his hand on my shoulder in a comforting gesture.

"The victim must be 50 pounds overweight."

"Fifty pounds? Are you sure?"

Burger chuckled. "I know shapely when I see it, and this girl is not. She's chunky. Go home, your roommate will show up, and hopefully, we'll find out who this Jane Doe is." The medical examiner paused. "Don't share this information with Hall, or I could lose my job."

I nodded. Leaving Burger, I looked at my watch. It was six-thirty. Mother would be livid. I had been roped into going over to her house for dinner, with her telling me she had great news to tell me.

I hopped into my car and burned rubber. If I was lucky, she would give me the silent treatment all evening, but Mother never missed a chance to zing me. She really got irritated when I maintained my composure, which I vowed to do tonight.

Speeding over to Mother's house, my mind wandered to Ronnie, my Mother's newest. They had met at an AA meeting. She had gotten into the sauce pretty well when Dad died. It seemed ironic at the time since Dad had been an alcoholic and treated her badly when he drank. She vowed never to touch the stuff. Mother hadn't had much of a life with Dad. Joan and I both knew that. However, in the end, when Dad was diagnosed with Cancer, they appeared to have come to a truce in their fighting and made the best of what was to be. Mother started going to Al-Anon. Dad stopped drinking and went to AA. When Dad died, Mother changed. She started dating right away.

I suppose she was lonesome, although Joan and I spent a lot of time with her. Once a dowdy dresser, she wore short skirts and tops exposing cleavage. Needless to say, she attracted men. Every night, she'd go bar hopping. Joan and I thought it was grief at first, and then we thought it might be a midlife crisis. We waited for her to change back to the Mother we knew, which wasn't that great, but at least we knew what we had to deal with. That hadn't happened so far. Mother met Ronnie at an AA meeting, but lately, I got the idea they don't go any longer, and sometimes I smelled liquor on Mother's breath. I was musing over this when a horn behind me broke my reverie. The light was green. I wasn't sure I was up to any news my Mother might have.

She didn't answer the door at first. She did that sometimes. On the third ring, she opened the door and stared at me.

"I couldn't help it," I said. "They found a girl's body,

and Shaw wanted me to get over there. It's a hot story for tomorrow's edition."

My Mother reluctantly moved aside so I could come into the house, but I felt her frozen stare on my back as I went into the living room. Ronnie was well on his way to feeling no pain. His eyes were red, and he weaved almost like he was dancing as he came over to me to kiss me on the lips. It was a wet, sloppy beer kiss. Ugh!

"We started without you since you didn't call," said Mother peevishly. Determined not to let her get me, I told her I was glad they had and sat on the couch. I wondered if I would hear her "good news" before or after I ate. I hoped after because I was hungry. Mother offered me some scallops wrapped in bacon. Hmmm, fancy.

"I made meatloaf, Ronnie's favorite," she told me again. As an aside, she added, "I know you like it too."

"Great." I moved towards the dining room, aware of the hunger noises emitting from me. They followed, my Mother, taking Ronnie's arm. I never liked it when I saw Ronnie sitting in Dad's spot at the head of the table, but I brushed my feelings off and concentrated on the meatloaf, mashed potatoes, salad, and broccoli. It was delicious, and I did it justice. Mother made a point of having to warm our plates up in the microwave. I tried to stay calm. I refused Mother's apple pie. She and Ronnie had two slices. Ronnie kept complimenting my Mother on the dinner until I thought I would gag. The freeloader never took my Mother out for an evening. She always cooked. I started to clear the dishes. My Mother asked me to stay put.

"We can do that later," she said. "Ronnie and I want to tell you our 'good news.'" I put on a false smile. Mother put her hand over Ronnie's. "You know that I have been very lonely since your Father died," she began.

Are they going to get married?

"I need something to occupy my time," she continued.

I nodded, hoping I looked encouraging.

"So, Ronnie and I are going to open up a health club."

A health club? Was she crazy?

"Yes. Ronnie's got some great ideas, and Sandy Ridge doesn't have anything but the YWCA, so this could bring the town up to speed with the rest of the world."

What could I say? Mother and Ronnie were excited.

"Err.......when do you anticipate this taking place? Have you thought this through? Who's going to run the club?"

"Well, Ronnie and I are looking at land now. Ronnie will hire trainers to work out with clients. His name has clout in the field with his winning competitions and all."

Yeah, how many years ago? I thought.

"I'll do the bookkeeping and be the receptionist. It will be fun." Mother rattled on.

Ronnie leaned across his plate and kissed my Mother.

"People are health conscious these days, but they need some direction to get in shape. That will be my job," he said proudly.

Does that mean they'll both stop drinking.?

Both Ronnie and my Mother looked at me expectantly. I thought frantically of what to say.

"You certainly have surprised me," Ronnie got up and poured another beer. He filled my Mother's wine glass. I told them I didn't know what to say. My Mother didn't notice my pensive look.

"Well, it will be a while yet before things get started. Ronnie wants to be sure the land we buy is in a good area with plenty of foot traffic and parking area."

"Yes, that would be important," I looked at my watch. "Oh, look at the time. I do have to get back to the newspaper. I'll just clear these things and put them in the dishwasher, and then I'll leave. You and Ronnie have so much to talk about."

I could hear the two chatting away in the dining room while I performed my task in the kitchen. They appeared to be oblivious to me, and when I returned to the dining room to say good night, Ronnie was kissing my Mother and fondling her breasts. I quickly left, the meatloaf turning sour in my stomach.

I rode to the newspaper in a rage. Hercules was going to tap Mother's money to finance what he wanted. Well, maybe Joan and I would have something to say about that. I wrote up the story about the murder. Phil Hodge had gotten great photographs. He had put them on my desk, and I quickly wrote. My mind with my Mother and her loser boyfriend. I finished. The story will be front page news tomorrow.

It was after one a. m. when I turned the key to my condo. I called Blaire's name outside her room. Nothing. I was bushed and crawled into bed. I had nightmares. All night long, I was chasing someone. When I caught up to the person, it was Mother. She was in workout gear.

CHAPTER 2

I was working on a story about a shooting at a local convenience store when Joan called the next day.

"Where were you, traitor?" I asked.

"Didn't Mom tell you? Timmy had a fever. His preschool called me yesterday and told me he wasn't feeling well. I picked him up early, so I thought it best not to take him out last evening."

When I asked about Doug, her husband, Joan said he had a school conference in the other part of the state. Doug was the superintendent of schools for York County.

"What's their good news?" asked Joan. "Are they getting married?" she joked.

"You won't believe it."

"They're getting married?" she yelled.

"No, no, calm down. They're opening a health club."

"What?"

"Yeah, do you believe it?" I could feel myself getting riled. The whole idea of Mother and Ronnie opening up a health club was ridiculous, and she was going to lose money.

"Joan, listen, can I call you later? I'm on deadline. I hung up from Joan when the telephone rang again. It was Ted, a police sergeant I dated. But I hadn't seen or talked to him for a week. He got to the point quickly.

"What are you doing tonight?"

"Nothing. You want to go out?" My words came out so quickly that I wanted to kick myself.

"I thought I could come over to your house, we'd order out, and we could watch wrestling."

Ugh, wrestling! Two men acting like jerks, throwing each other around. I was quiet.

"C'mon, Allison, there's a great match on tonight. We can snuggle on the couch, and I can explain wrestling to you. You'll love it."

I doubted that, but the thoughts of snuggling with Ted appealed to me.

"I work until six."

"I'll come around seven," said Ted. We decided on Italian. Ted would pick up two pizzas and an antipasto on the way to my townhouse. I hung up and finished my story. My attitude brightened at the prospect of seeing Ted. In the afternoon, I set up several interviews for stories. When I was leaving The Courier, I noticed Lacey Willis still working and wondered what her hours were because she was here when I came in the early morning and was still working when I left. I was curious about Lacey because she didn't seem to have any friends in the newspaper. Oh, people said hello and good night, but Lacey didn't appear to hang out with anyone. My instincts told me she was shy. Tonight, I vowed to find out more about her.

"You were here before me this morning, Lacey. Don't work so hard," I said.

The middle-aged woman looked tired.

"What are your hours?" I asked.

"I'm working late tonight. Shaw wants this story out, so I said I'd stay."

"Make sure he pays you overtime." We looked at each other and smiled. Shaw never paid overtime.

Passing Shaw's office to go home, I wondered if my editor had a life outside The Courier. The night crew was here, including the night editor. Shaw could go anytime now. Looking at my boss, I mused about how he must have been in his prime. Not bad looking,

Shaw must have had his chances with the women. What makes a guy change and be dull? Of course, I assumed Shaw was dull. At least he was to me. I'm not one to be subtle. Mother had always suggested this was one of my flaws. Shaw had been acting strange this week. He was bad-tempered, almost ugly to be around. Male menopause, probably.

I dropped by the police station to tell Police Chief Ed Hall about Blaire being missing. He took her description and said he'd put an APB out on her. He asked me what I knew about her. "Where she hangs out, what her interests are?"

Drat, why did he have to ask that?

"Chief, I was very naïve. She came into the newspaper. Shaw hired her. I was taking her around, introducing her to everyone. Blaire was extremely friendly, and when she mentioned she needed a place to stay, I suggested she stay with me. Looking back, she was very nervous about the meeting she was supposed to cover. I suspected she didn't have any reporter experience."

"Why would she say she did, then?"

"I don't know. An experienced reporter would already know the questions she asked. It was almost like she was trying to ingratiate herself with me."

I thought back to that night before Blaire went out to cover the Rod and Gun Club. She had said she was glad we were roommates because she could learn the newspaper business from me. That surprised me, and I told her I had worked at The Courier only a couple of years myself.

Hall was staring at me.

"Did you say something?" I asked.

"Yes, I was saying that you are friendly and personable," offered the Chief.

"Thanks. But, at one point, Blaire said she expected me to teach her about the job."

Hall shrugged. "That does sound strange. Why then would Shaw hire her?"

"Beats me," I said. "I just want to know if she's safe and if nothing too terrible has happened to her." I looked at my watch. It was six forty-five, and Ted was coming over at seven.

"I've got to run. Let me know if you hear anything." How could I forget Ted coming over? He'll be at my door and think I stood him up, and he'll leave. All kinds of scenarios went through my head as I broke the speed limit going home. In my frantic state, I dropped the keys to my door, tried to get inside, fumbled around a bit, and finally opened my front door. It was 6:55 pm. With five minutes to go, I threw off my work clothes, got into jeans and T-shirt, checked my hair, and put on fresh makeup. I got out the soda, ice, bucket, and hard liquor. Sometimes, Ted liked whiskey and water if he had a tough week.

He arrived at 7:15 with the pizzas, which smelled wonderful. I got a bowl for the salad.

"I'm starved," I said, reaching for a slice of pizza.

"There was a line. I hate to get take-out on Fridays." Ted looked for the remote and didn't find it.

"Geez, Allison, why can't you leave the remote on the TV where it belongs?" he asked, annoyed. Touchy, touchy. I lifted up some newspapers, found the remote, and handed it to him. Ted switched channels with a vengeance. I tossed the salad and put dishes and napkins on the coffee table.

"Damn, I missed the opening," he grunted.

"Take your jacket off, sit back, and eat," I said, trying to placate him.

He shushed me with his hand. Oh, great.

"Why don't you get cable?"

He looked at me. "I'm sorry, Allison," he said, planting a little kiss on my cheek. "I get so excited about wrestling. I forget myself sometimes. Come over here where I can put my arms around you." He hugged and kissed me hard. I succumbed to his strong arms and aftershave that I loved. He rested his head on my shoulder, turned, and again was mesmerized by the TV screen. I knew Ted was only interested in wrestling, but I kept hoping our relationship would be more, that our relationship would grow and be more than wrestling and drinking my booze. I got mad at myself for not taking more of a firm stand with him. The pizza called my name, and hunger for the pizza overcame me after realizing my hunger for Ted would not be satiated. I brought the pizza into the kitchen and chowed down. Ted didn't even notice I was gone. Dejected because I succumbed to the pizza, dejected because the guy on the couch didn't even know I wasn't in the room. I went to sit beside Ted. He was spurring his favorite wrestler on, shouting, flailing his arms around like a crazy person. What was it about wrestling that got guys so animated? I should excite Ted as much as those guys jumping around. Well, if you can't beat them, as the old cliché says.

I sat down next to Ted, figured out whom he was rooting for, and started yelling, too.

The next day, I called Burger to see if he had anything new on the murdered girl. Nothing. A week went by. The story faded from the front-page news. It had been ten days since the dead woman's body had been found. Shaw was riding everybody. He was angry, almost rageful, making demands. He must be cracking up.

Then, one slow afternoon, Burger called. Although the medical examiner had told me he would call when he knew something about the murdered girl, it surprised me to hear his voice that last day in September. Usually, he waited for me to bother him.

"You haven't called me today," he said jokingly.

"I thought I'd give you a break. Besides, you haven't had any info for me."

"I have now. You want to hear it?" I grabbed my pen. "Give."

"The girl died from persistent stab wounds. It's hard to say which ones killed her. I counted twenty-one over her entire body, mostly in the face."

"Any idea who she is and where she lives?" I could hear Burger shuffling some papers on his desk. "Blaire Nugent is the victim."

I almost dropped the telephone. "Blaire Nugent," I repeated. "But that can't be," I yelled on the telephone. "That's the name of my missing roommate."

Burger was silent. "It has to be her, then," he said with a sigh.

"But you said she was overweight."

"She is. Come over, identify the body, and see for yourself," said Burger.

"Ugh." I did not want to do that.

"It's the only way to know whether the body is that of your former roommate."

I hung up, gritting my teeth, having made arrangements to go to the medical examiner's office later. If the girl was Blaire Nugent, then who was my roommate? And why was she using someone else's name?

The afternoon was busy. At five o'clock, Shaw called me into his office.

"I want you in early next week for rewrites," he said without looking up from his desk. I nodded.

"What's new with the murdered girl they found a couple of weeks ago?" he asked. I told him about my conversation with Burger.

"It's the same girl that was your roommate?" he asked.

"There is some debate whether it is or not," I said. "The town's buzzing. I'm going over to Burger's office later to identify the body. I'm not looking forward to it."

Shaw said he wanted me to call him at home, whoever it was. He'd never said that before. I started to ask him why but noticed he appeared to be tense. The way he'd been blowing up, I didn't want another scene.

"Be sure you call me," Shaw repeated.

"I will, boss. Don't worry about it." What was his problem? Shaw shouldn't have given Blaire a hot issue like the Rod and Gun Club. But I felt guilty I hadn't helped her, maybe gone to the Selectmen's meeting with her, showing her the ropes. Shaw broke into my reverie.

"I thought you were leaving? I've got work to do, and I know you do." I left his office, grabbed my coat, drove very slowly to Burger's, and sat in my car. Did

I even have to do this? I shrugged my shoulders but knew I would regret passing up the opportunity.

Burger was writing at his desk. I knocked on the open door. He smiled up at me and pointed to the chair in front of it. We talked about trivialities for a while.

"Well, shall we?" Burger asked. Without a word, I followed the medical examiner out of the office into another, where there was a table draped with a sheet.

"This is going to be difficult," Burger said. "The body has been here for a week. Are you ready?"

"Let's get this over with."

Burger lifted the sheet. I looked at what I assumed must have been a pretty face. She was too short to be Blaire. I sighed, realizing I had been holding my breath.

"OK?"

"Yes," I said. "This woman is not the girl that was my roommate." Burger put the sheet over the body, and, in silence, we returned to his office. I shuddered. "I can't understand any of this," I said.

"What part of it?"

"Who is the woman that was my roommate, and what is her connection to that dead girl?"

"Time will provide all answers," summed up the medical examiner. "Hall wants a quick trial date. You'll be called as a material witness; did he tell you?"

"No. I don't know anything."

"Maybe you'll remember something by the time the trial begins. Do you want coffee?" I nodded. We didn't talk further about the body in the next room. The medical examiner appeared to want to calm me down before I left his office. Now that I knew I would be called a witness, how could I be? Calm, that is.

"Good coffee," I said, draining my cup. "Let me know if anybody claims the body." Burger agreed.

On the way home, I stopped at the police station. The sergeant on the desk was chatty. He announced me and indicated I should go into the Chief's office. Hall stood up when I entered. I'm glad there are a few gentlemen left.

"What can I do for you, ace reporter?"

"How come you didn't tell me I would be called a material witness in the murder of that girl? I didn't know her."

"But you did have a roommate who used the same name," said Hall. "Besides, that will be down the line. We have to find the murderer of that girl; we have to find your roommate and figure out what's going on."

"What do we know for sure?" I asked.

Hall shook his head. "Not too much. We've contacted the murdered girl's parents, and they are coming in from Quincy. Maybe we'll have more answers after we talk to them."

"When are they coming?"

"Tomorrow."

When I wanted to know what time the parents would be in Sandy Ridge. Hall didn't appear too thrilled.

"Chief, I have to interview them."

"After I do," said Hall.

"But of course," I smirked, walking toward the door.

"Allison, I don't want to throw you out of here again," said Hall.

Oh shit, why did Hall have to remind me of that? I thought, walking to my car. The humiliation of it all.

Shaw had almost fired me. I thought it was old news, and I tried hard not to remember it.

There was a money laundering scheme in Spencer, the next town over, and a coach at the Sandy Ridge High School was involved. He disappeared after his arraignment. I got a tip about where he was. I believed in his innocence, and it turned out he was, but before that became fact, Hall caught me searching the police log to find out what the cops knew since he was still on the lame. Lucky for me, the guy turned himself in to the police, but Hall accused me in the interim of interrogating his officers to find out facts. Actually, I was trying to find the coach's telephone number to get his side of things for a front-page story. He ended up calling me. He didn't want any publicity. I talked him into telling me his side of the story if he was innocent like he said he was. He turned himself in the same day as the newspaper ran my story. Hall was furious, said I was interfering with police, and for weeks would not let me get a look at the police log. Shaw had to get a stringer to cover the police log for a month. Hall did not accept my apology and called me a "hotshot reporter." His tone was sarcastic and mocking, putting me in my place.

In time, his attitude lightened. He still can call me "hot shot reporter" sometimes when I get too full of myself. It took me a long time to get into Hall's good graces again. I did it by confidentially telling him tips I had heard around town that turned out to be true.

Ugh, I didn't want to live through that again. Remembering my faux paus with Hall broke me out in a sweat inside the station. The cool air outside hit me like air conditioning on an August day.

"Allison, Allison," came Hall's voice. The Chief was dangling my keys in front of him. "Where's my mind," I said, grabbing them. Looking at them, I had an epiphany.

"What now?"

"Ed, I just realized my former roommate still has her key to my condo."

"Get the locks changed."

I looked at my watch. "Too late now. I'll call them in the morning."

I was mad at myself for not thinking about the keys earlier. On the way home, I grabbed a burger and fries from my favorite fast-food restaurant as I drove into my condo parking lot. I noticed someone had parked in my assigned space. Damn, there is a sign right in front saying that residents have lettered parking, and the visitor's parking is in the next lot. All residents were in their spots, so it had to be someone visiting. This happens a lot because the visitor's parking spots are further away, and people are lazy. I was grumpy. Actually, I was pissed. But then I realized I could park in Sue's spot since she was working a double shift as a nurse in a Portland hospital and wouldn't be home until tomorrow. Sue was my neighbor where my cat Muffy was treated royally. Tomorrow, I would be at work by the time Sue came home. I carried my fast food into my condo, feeling my way over to the other side of the room for the light. I do have to get a light bulb for the lamp by the door instead of feeling myself along to the other side of the room. I do have to write these things down. Otherwise, I never remember, especially now with this murder. The food smells were overcoming my taste buds. Muffy nuzzled up to me, but I got a plate from the kitchen and consumed the food like it was my last meal. Muffy was still rubbing against me. I picked her up and burrowed my nose in her fur.

"Will you protect me in case my roommate comes back, Muffy?" My cat looked greedily at the scrapes left of my food. "Sure, Muffy, we know where your heart lies." I put her down and went to the cupboard to get a catnip. That should keep her happy for a while. On the way to my bedroom, I stopped at Blaire's door and listened. Silence. Once in my bedroom, I put on my pajamas. It was early, but I was tired, and a book would lull me to sleep. Before retiring, I tried the locks to my apartment three times. I told myself I was becoming my Mother with the OCD actions, but I did it anyway. They say you do turn into your Mother in your later years, your face, your actions. I could only hope that wasn't so. I finished the book I was reading and still couldn't sleep, so I made myself an Orange Mandarin cup of tea and returned to my bedroom, searching the shelves for another book. It's funny how your mind can play tricks on you. I'd never noticed the squeaks in my floorboards before. It wasn't long before I realized I couldn't concentrate. I scanned my bedroom TV. Why isn't there more on cable? Now, I was wide awake. I went to check the front door again and flipped on my answering machine. My Mother's excited voice was telling me about the land she and Ronnie had found for their health club. Not tonight. Like Scarlett O'Hara, I would worry about that tomorrow.

Chapter 3

I went back to bed and must have slept for an hour or so, but when I awoke, I couldn't get back to sleep. I got up, went out to the living room and sat. It had not been a pretty sight to look at the dead girl in the morgue. Her image would stay with me for a long time, and I could not comprehend why anyone could kill another.

I thought back to the night my roommate went to that meeting. I felt guilty now that I hadn't gone with her. Perhaps things would have been different. But I knew that if anyone wanted to kill a person, they would be killed sooner or later. My going to that meeting with her would have only prolonged her death, or maybe it would have quickened mine. If I had canceled my date and gone with her, could I have helped her? Maybe I should take Judo or learn tricks to protect myself?

And what's with the two girls with the same name.? Who was my roommate? Was the dead girl and my roommate related? I figured someone had followed both girls to Sandy Ridge. But what was their connection, and why come to Sandy Ridge? I conjured up several scenarios in my mind.

Finally, knowing I wasn't getting anywhere, I started for my bedroom and stopped outside Blaire's door. Why not pack up things and put them downstairs in the storage area? Was that a good idea? Suppose she came back and didn't like what I did with her things? Should I do something like that? It's funny how your mind plays tricks with you sometimes. The squeaks in my floorboard reverberated as I walked. I kept going back to check the doors. Maybe I should get a security system. Chiding myself, I went to the kitchen, got some milk, warmed it up, and returned to my bedroom. I was being silly. Truth be known, I wanted to snoop around her room. Ed Hall said he wanted to look through my roommate's things. I would simply help him out. It wasn't a crime scene, after all. Not yet. It hadn't been proven my roommate, who I knew as Blaire, killed anyone.

Thoroughly convincing myself of my pure intentions, I set the warm milk aside and entered the girl's room slowly and carefully. My roommate hadn't unpacked completely. She had books and personal items on the bureau. Her bed was made. I stripped it, folding sheets and one blanket. I took her deodorant, hair spray, face cream, and cologne and looked for a place to put them. Curiosity got the best of me. I started looking through each box, starting with the smaller ones, working up to the larger ones, and putting items in as space allowed. It looked like she was a pack rat. I could identify with all the papers, newspapers, and magazines cluttering up the condo. I told myself that I would read these things when I had time, but they just kept accumulating, and I kept moving them from place to place. With Blaire's things downstairs, I could use this room for my junk.

Blaire had term papers from high school and college. I found what I thought looked like love letters tied together with a pink ribbon. Cute! I was tempted to read them but decided against it. Thoughts of Ted came into mind. He certainly wasn't the type to write love letters. Thinking of Ted made me feel lousy. Where was our relationship going?

Knock it off, Allison. Get busy with the task ahead. If I organized the contents better, I could put the sheets and blanket on the bottom of this large box, and that would cushion the souvenirs and picture frames. I took everything out, put the bedding in the bottom, and one by one, put the other things back. I was impressed with how neat I was being. Never would I be so meticulous with my own stuff.

If I was honest with myself, I was a reporter looking for a scoop ahead of the police.

At the bottom of a box was a hand diary, the type that had a calendar and a place for telephone numbers. It was for the year 1993. Geez, she did save everything. This was boring. It was eleven o'clock. If I fell asleep right away, I might still get enough shut-eye. Should I lock her door so that even if she came back when I was away, my roommate couldn't get in and get her things? Now, Allison, why would you do that? I didn't want to mess with her, especially after I thought of what Hall had said earlier about her being Blaire Nugent's killer. A shiver went through my body. I willed the thought out of my mind but did go to double-check whether the doors were locked again. I did look through the diary, but it was dull, so I threw it in with the rest of the stuff. When I did, the corner of a newspaper clipping became exposed in the box. For some reason, I reached in and got it. It was a short story with several pictures of what looked like a dinner being held at a hotel. I became riveted by what I saw in front of me.

He was younger, but the picture in front of me definitely was Bill Shaw. I hadn't lived in Sandy Ridge at the time, but the veteran reporters at the newspaper had told me about it. Shaw had a huge plaque on his wall, also. I looked at the date. Ten years ago. It had to be the same. Shaw received the "Best Editor of a Small Town" award from Artists

Publishing, which owned The Courier as well as other newspapers in Maine. The award banquet received national attention from the press because Artists Publishing has its main publishing house in New York. In fact, Shaw received the award in New York.

In the back row of the picture was my roommate. That proved she knew Shaw years before. The article must have appeared in a Boston newspaper since Blaire was from the area unless she subscribed to the New York Times. There was no way of knowing since the date and newspaper imprint were not at the top of the story. What if she had lied about being from Boston? If she took someone else's name, she wouldn't hesitate to do anything else. Certainly not if she's a murderer.

I took the clipping and went back to my bedroom. I stashed it on my bedside table, shut off the light, and lay there wondering what the connection could be between her and Shaw. Had she followed Shaw to Sandy Ridge?

The next thing I knew, my alarm clock was buzzing, and the sun was pouring through my window.

CHAPTER 4

In my hurry to get to work the next day, I forgot the clipping until I saw Shaw. He hadn't changed much in ten years. He had a few more bags under his eyes. I couldn't tell in the picture whether he had the paunch he did now. I averaged him to be in his late fifties. In his younger years, he might have been considered attractive. I didn't know anything about his personal life, whether or not he had been married. The way he was acting lately, who would have him? Today, he was in a foul mood, yelling and demanding everyone jump. Shaw was systematically calling each reporter into his office and complaining about their work. Most would come out looking dejected, shoulders and heads down. I tried to keep busy, but holding my breath, waiting for my turn at bat. Miraculously, it didn't come. I stayed out of Shaw's way through the morning, writing up the story of Sandy Ridge's first homicide in years and how the murdered girl had the same name as another newcomer to our seaside community. But my turn with Shaw came after lunch.

"Allison, get in here," he shouted. Uh, oh.

"That story on the murdered girl was lousy," he said.

"What was wrong with it?" I asked, getting pissed.

"It was confusing," he answered.

"Boss, the whole case is confusing. I told you that last night when I called you. I had a roommate that has disappeared. She has the same name as the girl who was murdered. Police are investigating."

"Does Hall have any clues in the case?" asked Shaw. "No," I said, talking louder. "That's why it is a puzzling case. The young woman was not from the area. The murdered girl's name is correct. Police traced her fingerprints. There's no doubt about that. The question is, why did my roommate take her name?"

"Maybe not," said Shaw.

"What?"

"Maybe it's just a weird coincidence," said Shaw. "Maybe the girls didn't even know each other. I still say your roommate found a honey and is shacking up somewhere. She'll surface when she's ready."

Was he cracking up?

Shaw looked down at the papers on his desk. That was my cue to leave, which I did. At the door, I turned. "Boss, can I ask you a question?"

He didn't even raise his head. "Yeah?"

"Why did you hire the girl I knew as Blaire?"

"Because she needed a job," Shaw barked. "Isn't that why I hired you?"

I came back and sat in the seat. "I just got the feeling she didn't have any journalism experience, that's all."

"On the contrary, smart ass. She had references. I called the newspaper in Massachusetts, where she had been a reporter, and they had high praise for her. Anyway, don't get off track. Don't slouch off on your research, or you'll be out of here," my editor said, pointing his finger at me and shooing me out of his office. I left him to his thoughts and returned to my desk to continue working on a feature for Sunday's edition.

A woman in town was celebrating her ninety-seventh birthday. She sounded sweet on the phone, inviting me to her party at the town's nursing home. I begged off but did send a photographer to get good shots to accompany the story. The woman had seven children, twelve grandchildren, and five great-grandchildren, all of whom gave me great anecdotes about the woman who had been prominent in local politics at the turn of the century.

Shaw always stayed in my gut whenever we had words. Maybe I should start looking for another job. A friend in Portland said the daily there was looking for staff reporters. Life in the big city could be fun. Deep in thought, I walked to the front door, passing Lacey's office. She was beginning to leave. I asked her to join me for dinner.

"I was only going home and getting fast food on the way. You'd be doing my digestion a favor if you ate with me, and I would enjoy the company," I said.

Lacey smiled, and I realized it was the first time I had seen her do so. The woman had a dimple in the hollow of her right cheek, hazel eyes brightened her entire face, and she had white teeth that didn't look like she had whitened them but were natural.

"I'd like that," she said. Together, we passed Shaw's office without a glance. We were teenagers sneaking past our parents to go to meet friends.

Outside, Lacey's shoulders relaxed. "I thought for sure he'd catch us," she said. We didn't talk further until we were in the diner, and the waitress had given us menus. When she had, I asked Lacey how long she had worked at The Courier. She thought for a moment. "It must be twelve years now." She shook her head. "I can't believe it's been that long."

The waitress came over and set down water. We ordered coffee and asked for a few minutes to look at the menu.

"How was Shaw in those days?" I asked.

"I've never seen him as moody or touchy as recently." Lacey surveyed the menu and looked over at me. "I can't figure him out. Can you?"

"Damned if I know. Tell me about those early days. What was he like?"

"The Courier was a good newspaper. That's why I wanted to work at it. I admired the way he operated his newsroom. He had a good relationship with his staff. His nature was such that everyone wanted to please him. Nowadays, he's unreasonable and acts like a bear. My friend told me the scuttlebutt around the newspaper was that reporters wanted to leave."

"I've been thinking the same thing," I added.

"He's going to lose his best people," she said.

I told Lacey how Shaw had chewed me out today about my story on the murder. "There isn't much to report. I can't conjure up facts where there aren't any."

"What's he want you to do?"

"Shaw wants this murder solved. He thinks my roommate found a honey and will come back to the newspaper when she wants to and that her disappearance doesn't have anything to do with the murder."

I didn't tell Lacey about the clipping I discovered last night. I was reluctant to share that with anyone yet.

"You often work late?" I asked. "Why?"

"Shaw asks me to do things at the last minute. He says he wants it right away." The woman suddenly looked tired.

"Lacey, do you belong to the Union?

"I can't afford to belong," she said.

"You can't afford not to belong," I said. "Stop acting like a slave to Shaw. He's taking advantage of you. You're in here for too many hours and without overtime."

Lacey put up her hands. "He asks me, what can I say?"

"What part of 'no' don't you think he'll understand?" I asked. "The work will be there tomorrow."

My stomach growled. My friend didn't seem to notice. I asked Lacey what Shaw was like when she first came to the newspaper.

Lacey conceded she admired the way Shaw had brought the newspaper from a paper with little news to a contender for the most circulation in the state.

"He wanted every detail of a story to be exact. Nowadays, he's unreasonable and like a bear." My stomach growled again. We both heard it and laughed. "Let's order," I said. Lacey ordered another coffee and a side salad.

"Is that all you're having," I asked. The girl could stand to gain a few pounds. Silence. Then Lacey bent over the table as if in a whisper. "I'm short of cash tonight."

"I'll lend you money," I said. "Order a full meal." My friend told me she wasn't hungry. I made a mental note to pick up the tab. When the waitress came, I ordered a cheeseburger with lettuce, tomato, and fries.

There was an awkward pause. The waitress left to fill our orders.

"Tell me, Lacey, are you married?" I didn't see a wedding band, but one never knows.

"I'm divorced. Never had any children. I live with my Dad now. He has Parkinson's disease, and I'll probably have to put him in a nursing home soon. I just don't know how I'll be able to afford it, so I'm thinking I'll just take care of him at home."

I asked her if her Dad could be left alone. "Who takes care of him when you're at work?" Lacy said she has a woman come every day.

"I'm sorry about your situation. All the more reason why you should get compensated for the extra hours you put in. Speak to Shaw and tell him about your circumstances." Lacey told me our editor already knew.

Shaw's a jerk, I thought. My burger and fries came with Lacey's salad. We ate in silence for a few minutes. I gave her some of my fries. She ate them without a word. I suspected Lacey knew a lot more than she let on about the workings at the newspaper and Shaw. I would have to wait for another time since I didn't want to make my new friend nervous. I sensed Lacey needed a friend, and I could use one myself. I told Lacey again about getting chewed out on the story I did on the recent murder.

"I'm not sure how much more I should take," I said.

"Isn't it odd about the new reporter who didn't show up for work the next day?" I asked. "And she hasn't been seen since. I know the meetings are tough, but that's carrying it to extremes."

"That is strange," Lacey said as she poured more dressing on her salad. "Shaw acted so weird around her."

My antenna was up. "What do you mean?"

"I went to his office while she was there for the job interview. I wanted him to approve my copy. He had a look on his face like he had been caught with his hand in the cookie jar. She looked like she had been crying. He told me to leave."

My mind went back to the newspaper clipping I had discovered. What Lacey said only cemented my suspicions that Shaw and my roommate knew each other before the girl came to Sandy Ridge. It looked like she had come to find Shaw. In my mind, I still called my former roommate Blaire because I didn't know what to call her.

Chapter 5

The following day, before going to work, I went on an interview about a pharmacy closing after twenty years. Once at my desk, I opened my mail. There was an amended notice of the public hearing request for a full-time liquor license for the Rod and Gun Club. The meeting was going to be next Tuesday. That was the meeting the girl who called herself Blaire was supposed to cover. Sometime before, during, or after that meeting, she disappeared. Did something happen at the meeting that made her leave? Did someone there make her leave? Or did they take her by force?

The Rod and Gun Club came out of obscurity within the last five years. Before that, the club maintained a quiet existence; it was a small building west of the center of town at the end of a residential street. It was surrounded by woods.

Inside was a dining area with tables, chairs, and a snack bar. A bigger room had a dance floor and another bar. I never knew anyone who was a member, but I was fairly new to Sandy Ridge. Now, the club had a new owner, Sam Davis, who wanted to build on to the club. He wanted to enlarge the dance area and put another bar on the other side of the room. A full kitchen would be installed in the dining room, eliminating the snack bar. Davis also wanted the addition to be a function room. So, Davis wanted to spend money he hoped would bring an even bigger return, thanks to the many industrial parks and big-name companies that were settling off the Maine Turnpike close to our town.

The liquor license issue could tear this small town apart. There were pros and cons on both sides, and I believed the people involved were good people who wanted to do right by the town. No matter how Selectmen voted, it would be front-page news the next day.

By early afternoon, I had caught up with my work and decided to call Mother. In retrospect, I can't imagine why. She is so full of herself. I keep thinking each time will be different, but it never is. This call was Mother, as always, chatting nonstop about the land she and Ronnie were thinking of buying for the health club. She called it "perfect."

"How many parcels of land have you looked at?" I asked. "Are you meeting with any developers?"

Mother acknowledged she and her boyfriend had not called any developers, and the one parcel of land was the only one they had looked at.

I told her to make a list of perks she and Ronnie wanted, such as ample parking. They also should know what kind of building they need and how many square feet. How many rooms did they want? Would there be a reception area?

Where would the showers, sauna, and all the other things health clubs usually have be located? That's why they needed an architect.

"You have a lot of work to do yet before actually buying the land," I said. My Mother admitted I was right. I was on a roll, so I told her she and Ronnie needed to appear knowledgeable when they were dealing with the companies that would be doing the work.

She didn't interrupt, and I could hear a screeching of a pen-like she was taking notes on what I was telling her. My Mother asked me a few questions and actually let me talk, which surprised me. Usually, I had to talk fast with her if I wanted to get my point across.

I called Joan after Mother and recounted my conversation with her.

"What do you think?" I asked. "Mother seems so happy. Yet, I can't help but think Ronnie is using her.

Not to mention the fact that she knows nothing about health clubs and has tried to avoid them all her life."

"Who knows," my sister said. "Let's see what happens." We talked for a while, and before saying goodbye, she asked, "Any news about your roommate?"

"No. I'm gathering her belongings and putting them down in my storage area for now."

"Any theories on what happened?"

Out of the corner of my eye, I saw Shaw coming my way. "Nope, got to go."

"Keep me posted," said Joan and hung up.

Shaw came over to my desk and gave me a paper. It was a duplicate copy of the change in the Selectmen's meeting. "I already got one."

"Well, throw one away," Shaw said with a shrug. My boss didn't like personal calls from the office, and I felt guilty, sensing he knew I called Mother and my sister. I pretended to study something on my desk. Shaw walked away. I glanced at the clock. Time to go home. I spotted Lacey straightening up her desk and went over to her.

"Leaving for the evening?"

She smiled. "I'm taking your advice."

"Good. I'll walk out with you."

We parted company at the garage. I drove home feeling good about my day since there were some good stories of mine running in the newspaper this week.

Once inside my condo, I threw my coat and purse on the armchair and went into the kitchen. Tonight's dinner was going to be a Hamburg. I made a patty, put a potato in, and got out salad fixings. While getting the food out, I put in a new box of Baking Soda, ran a sponge over the spills, and took out leftovers I no longer recognized.

It took me little time, and soon, I was eating, feeling pretty pleased with myself for being somewhat domestic. And I wondered why I didn't go domestic more often.

Afterward, I put the unused Hamburg in a container, glad that any decision for meals had been decided for the week ahead. I grabbed an apple to munch on as I looked at the TV listings. There was a program on Elizabeth Barrett Browning. I enjoyed trying my hand at poetry, and Browning had been a favorite of mine in college. But after ten minutes, I grew tired of hearing about "Liz" and turned to reruns of "Law and Order."

I soon turned the TV off and decided to start a library book written by my favorite mystery author. It was on my bedside table. Or I thought so. But it wasn't. I looked under the bed in case it had fallen. I opened the night table. Things appeared to be in disarray. It was then I remembered the news clipping of Shaw I found in Blaire's room. I had put it in my end table. Methodically, I took everything out of it. The clipping was not there. I sat on my bed to think. What could have happened to the clipping? And my library book? All of a sudden, lightning struck. I rushed into my roommate's room. It was empty. Boxes were gone. I looked in her closet. Empty. A hat box on the top shelf of the closet that was full of my Christmas ornaments was torn, and bulbs were hanging from bare coat hangers. The shoes thrown on the floor of the closet haphazardly weren't there. It was as if nobody had occupied the room. But I knew better. In a corner of the room, on the windowsill, was my library book.

Chapter 6

My roommate, who had disappeared, had been in my condo. Panic rose in me; suppose she was still here? Don't be silly, I told myself. If she was here, I would know it by now. However, I searched my closet and looked under the long dresses. I opened my bureau drawers. Everything was scattered. The papers in my bottom drawer were disheveled. I searched her room again.

How long had I been out of my condo? All day. She could have been watching, and when I left for work, she came in and took her belongings. And, the clipping that was in my end table? How did she know I had found it? My roommate must have had someone to help her move out, but that meant that she knew someone in town who assisted her. Then, another thought hit me. Suppose it wasn't her who had ransacked my place? Well, ransacked was too strong a word. Pilfering indiscriminately would be a better way of putting it.

I looked at the clock. It was nine p.m. I knew I couldn't stay in my place alone tonight. I reached for the telephone and called Ted. When the answering machine came on, I hung up and called police headquarters.

I hadn't realized I was so upset until I heard a voice coming from my end of the line that sounded like someone else.

"Ted, I'm so glad you're working."

"Allison, what's wrong? You sound terrible."

"My roommate came back and took all her belongings while I was at work."

"What's so bad about that?"

Men are so dense. "I don't want a possible murderer roaming around my condo."

"Get the locks changed," he retorted.

"You're pissing me off," I shouted into the phone. "I can't get them changed until tomorrow, which I intend to do. Tell me something I don't know."

Ted was quiet and then asked me what I wanted him to do. "What can I say that will make you calm?"

I took a long breath before I answered. "I'm afraid she will come back. I'm afraid she killed that girl in the woods." Please, God, let me sound coherent.

"Can you come over here after work and stay the night? I don't want to be alone."

"Sure, I guess I could. I'll go home, get a change of clothes for tomorrow, and be over to your place around midnight."

"Great," I said, feeling better. "I'll see you then."

A few minutes off the phone, I chided myself. I had sounded like a hysterical woman, not the capable professional I wanted everyone to think I was. Ted must have thought I was losing it. Come to think of it, I was. I needed a drink.

I poured myself a Scotch. Ugh! How can people drink that? I debated whether to have water or ginger ale. I eyed the cake on the kitchen counter, which, compulsively, I had whittled down one slice at a time. It called to me now. I had second thoughts about having asked Ted to stay the night. Where had my pride been? I finished my drink, made another, and turned on the TV. I took a blanket out of the closet, put it over me, laid down on the couch, and fell asleep immediately. The downstairs buzzer jolted me awake. Who could it be? Then I remembered. The sound of his voice comforted me as I buzzed Ted in.

"Geez, Allison, you look awful," was Ted's greeting as I opened the door.

Ted was always a diplomat.

"I fell asleep, wise guy. Come on in. Want a drink?"

I never saw Ted refuse a drink. It wasn't tonight, either. I poured him his usual scotch and water. I refilled mine.

"Drop your things on the chair. I'll get you sheets and a blanket." I ignored his disappointed look.

"C'mon, let's sit on the couch and talk about what happened today," he suggested.

I began slowly telling him about looking for my library book this evening and not finding it, discovering my end table had been rifled, as well as my bureau. It was then I had the idea of looking in my former roommate's room. Her clothes and boxes to be unpacked were gone when I went into her room. My library book was on the window sill.

"Allison, sometimes I don't understand you. Why didn't you get the locks changed when she didn't show up after a few days? Then, a murdered girl is discovered that has the same name as your roommate, and we know there has to be a connection. What about this doesn't cause you to think you should have your locks changed?"

"Are you here to protect me or find fault with me?" I told him that I hadn't thought of it until today. "It's been busy at the newspaper with the murder. Shaw is spastic."

Ted told me to tell Hall first thing in the morning about the girl's things being taken out of my apartment. "Meanwhile, I'm here to protect you," said Ted. "Relax. Let's watch TV."

"I'm going to bed."

"C'mon, let's cuddle." We sat on the couch. Ted put his arm around me and drew me close while flicking channels. He decided on the Late Show.

I finished my drink. His was empty, and he got up to get another. He asked me if I wanted more.

"Sure," I said, feeling mellow.

Ted came back and put his feet up on the ottoman. It was a peaceful scene I was enjoying. Ted leaned over and kissed me, and I melted into his arms. He grabbed my breasts, and I held them up to him. When I felt his hands under my shirt, I quivered, and his tongue sought mine with new urgency. He unhooked my bra, and I laid back on the couch. His legs straddled mine. His kisses were hurting me now. Ted forced himself between my legs, and I quivered at his arousal. He tugged at my underpants, and I arched my back to help him. That's when I hit my elbow on the coffee table. I heard the sound of glass breaking as pain seared my elbow.

"What the hell……."

"I looked down. My arm was in the middle of broken shards of glass, which were once my coffee table. Blood was gushing out.

Ted jumped up. "Are you alright?"

"Quick, get me a towel from the kitchen."

I sat up. My whole arm was throbbing painfully. Ted came back. "Press this as tight as you can to the area."

I did as Ted told me. Man, there was a lot of blood spurting out. After what seemed like a long time, the blood was not subsiding. Ted said we should go to the hospital. I grabbed two towels, and we left.

Neither of us spoke in the car. I was trying to keep the blood off Ted's upholstery. He was driving fast. Maybe he knew something I didn't. When we got to the hospital entrance, Ted took a left and dropped me off at the ER entrance.

"I'll park the car. You go in."

I did as I was told and explained my situation to the receptionist on duty. She directed me to an <u>area</u>

where, after ten minutes, a woman came and asked me what kind of insurance I had. She asked me questions, and I filled in endless forms, after which she told me to have a seat and the doctor would see me shortly.

By now, my towel was saturated with blood, and I asked for another, which the receptionist went and got for me. Ted had joined me by then, and we sat down to wait.

After a half hour, Ted asked if I wanted coffee out of the vending machine. I said no, and he went to get one. When he did return, it was to throw the coffee, cup, and all into the nearest trash container. I picked up a copy of People Magazine. Surprisingly, it was a recent one. I sat back and waited for my name to be called.

After several hours, Ted was getting restless. So was I.

"I think I'll go and ask how much longer before we're taken," he said. I nodded. By now, the ER was full. People were coughing, sleeping, and pacing the floor. By the look of my towel, I would need a transfusion.

"I need help," I said, rushing over to the receptionist. "My arm won't stop bleeding."

A cute guy in green scrubs came out, and I turned my attention to him telling my story. He took a look at my arm and looked at the receptionist. She gave us a blank stare. "Come with me," he said.

I turned to Ted. He was reading my magazine.

I followed the medic, who introduced himself as Jake. He directed me to an empty hospital bed and pulled the curtain around us.

"What seems to be the problem?"

Wasn't it obvious? "I hurt my elbow on my coffee table."

Jake took the towel away and studied my elbow. He turned it over.

"Ouch." I couldn't read his expression, but I did know the pain was bad without him telling me.

"That's quite a cut you have there." This guy was brilliant. He turned to a cart in back of him, got a thermometer, and stuck it under my tongue. When it beeped, he turned and made a notation. Then he got the blood pressure cuff and put it on me. He stepped back while the blood pressure machine squeezed my upper arm tightly until I cried out in pain. Jake dislodged my pressure cuff.

"Sorry, it has to be that tight to get a good reading," he said. He made another notation. Jake then told me the doctor would be in to see me soon. When he left, I laid down on the bed. My elbow was throbbing. It was quarter to three in the morning. Bleeding, tired, and hungry, that was me.

I dozed for a while. A noise from the next bed woke me. It was four-thirty. Where the hell was the doctor? Did Ted go home? Why hadn't he joined me in the room? The curtain moved, and a short, stocky, red-cheeked man entered in a lab coat.

"Hello, I'm Dr. Stillwell. I understand you hurt your elbow on a coffee table last night."

"Yes, I did."

He looked at my injury. "How did you do this?" he asked, his face tightening in concentration as he examined my arm.

I could feel myself blushing and mumbling something about putting a hot coffee pot on the glass, and it broke. The doctor spent some time prodding and pressing the area. He called for a nurse.

"There are some particles of glass in your elbow," the doctor explained. "We are going to clean it out, but it may hurt while we're doing it."

I nodded sympathetically at what he and the nurse were having to do. My elbow burned. There were a lot of little pieces of glass. I tried looking the other way, but yes, it hurt like hell. The doctor used tweezers and put the glass pieces on a gauze. I felt weak and nauseous at the same time.

"You had quite a bit of glass in there. It went into some muscle tissue; that's why it bled so badly, but I think it's under control now. I'll give you a prescription for the pain."

He handed me a salve. "Put this on four times a day. My nurse will dress the wound now, but tomorrow, wash the elbow with antiseptic soap, put the salve on, and wrap it up. Follow up with your primary physician next week."

The nurse wrapped my elbow and warned me not to bend it. How does one do that? I wanted to ask her, but she left, and I needed to get out of there. I followed the nurse out to the reception area. By now, there were new people sleeping in chairs. Ted was one of them. I nudged him and motioned to my elbow.

"Let's go home."

Ted got up and stretched. "How long have we been here?"

"Forever."

It hurt like hell to put on my coat. I followed Ted out. "It's cold." I shivered.

"Yeah," Ted said, trudging toward his car. He did not look happy. I refrained from talking. I wasn't exactly thrilled to be in a hospital parking lot at 5 a.m. myself.

Once in the car, I wanted to fall asleep, but Ted didn't look too wide awake. How could a night that looked so promising turn out so bad? We saw no one on the road driving home. My condo looked eerie, illuminated only by lamplight. There was an unfamiliar stillness in the air that permeated my body and vibrated negative forces through it.

When I turned the key to my condo, I immediately headed for a chair, where I collapsed.

"I'll lay down on the couch for an hour or two," said Ted. "Then I'll shower, get dressed and go to work."

"Thanks for coming to the hospital with me," I said. He kissed me lightly. "I was glad to be of service."

Chapter 7

I took a pain pill and got into bed. My sleep was fragmented because I'd turn over and wake up from the pain of my elbow.

The next day, I slept late. Ted had gone. As hot as I was for the guy, I didn't want to deal with him today.

When I called Shaw, he reminded me of how little sick leave I had. "Today's a busy day. You know we're shorthanded."

Shaw has such a good personality.

I hung up from him, took a pain pill, made myself a cup of coffee and went back to bed. Propping up my pillows, the day loomed ahead of me. I called Chief of Police Ed Hall and told him about Blaire coming back to the condo and taking her things while I was at work.

"Are you sure it was her?" he asked.

"I can't be sure of anything, chief, but who else would want her clothes? I'm getting my locks changed today."

"That's a good idea."

I was tempted to tell him about the newspaper clipping with Shaw's picture that I had found in Blaire's room, but I wanted to confront Shaw himself. I liked the guy enough that I didn't want him to get into trouble.

After I hung up from Hall, I called the locksmith. He said he'd be at my house between three and five p.m. My eyes were heavy. I laid out on my bed and slept for a couple of hours.

The telephone woke me. It was Ted.

"How are you feeling?"

"Like a bulldozer rolled over me."

"Glad you haven't lost your sense of humor," he said. We talked for a few minutes, after which I took a shower. My arm was supposed to be kept straight. The pain was bad. Getting dressed was worse. It took me a long time to put on jeans and a sweatshirt. I needed to get the prescription filled for my elbow, but that would have to wait until the locksmith left.

The owner himself came at exactly three o'clock. Two hundred fifty dollars later, I was on my way to the pharmacy. My elbow hurt like hell.

The pharmacy said my meds would take twenty minutes. Might as well go over to MacDonald's to fortify myself. Upon returning to get my prescription, I spied Burt Olsen. I darted down another aisle. After stuffing myself with a strawberry shake, fries and a Whopper, I didn't want to talk politics tonight. Oh, Oh…….

"Great story you did on our meeting coming up Tuesday," he said enthusiastically from a couple of aisles over. He came closer. Oh, Lord, I thought. I don't want to rehash this with him tonight. I looked over at the pharmacists, hoping they would call my name. Again, he reiterated the importance of the Rod and Gun Club not getting their continuous liquor license. He told me the same stories over and over. My eyes pleaded with the cashier to call my name. In time, they did. I paid by credit card.

"It will be interesting to see how things shape up Tuesday," was my fleeting remark to Olsen.

On the way out, I got gauze and grabbed a couple of chocolate bars that said they were two for five dollars. What a bargain! I paid for my new purchases at the front, where a thin, older woman with half glasses rang them up. Once in the car, I opened one of the candy bars and ate it driving home. It tasted lousy. I threw both in the trash.

Once home, I washed my prescription down with Diet Coke, threw a potato in the oven, nuked a piece of frozen salmon and cooked some frozen vegetables.

I washed my elbow, put salve on it, wrapped it up again, and when my meal was ready, ate it hardheartedly. Muffy stationed herself right in front of me under the table, hoping I would drop some food down to her, either accidentally or on purpose. After washing the dishes, I called it an early night and got a reasonably good sleep.

The next morning, I went to work, but I was late because it took me forever to get dressed. It was just my luck. Shaw was rushing out of his office as I was sneaking in.

"Nice of you to join us."

"Sorry I'm late, but I hurt my elbow, and it's difficult to get dressed since I'm not supposed to bend it."

Was Shaw sympathetic? What do you think?

"Yesterday we really needed you, and today has been a horror show so far."

Thanks for your concern, I thought.

The newsroom remained hectic all day. The morning was busy because we had hired two new correspondents who had sent stories in last night that had to be redone. I had to call people quoted in the story and confirm facts. We had a ten-thirty deadline. It was difficult for me to type; it was awkward and painful.

I asked Shaw why correspondents, when they are hired, are not trained to some degree.

"You want to do it?" he asked.

"Yes, if it means staff people don't have to rewrite at the last moment," I said.

"Gripe, gripe, gripe, that's all you know how to do." Didn't Shaw care anymore? He had gotten everything in on the deadline. He wouldn't worry until the next time. He didn't care that my elbow was killing me. Those pain pills were good for nothing. Maybe I should take two at a time? Maybe I would feel better.

Chapter 8

At noon, Lacey came over to my desk to tell me she missed me yesterday and to ask me if I was free for lunch.

"Oh yes, let's go now before I throw something at Shaw."

Lacey and I decided to go to the diner we had gone the first time. I took a pain pill with a glass of water and ordered a salad. Lacey ordered the same.

"How's your father?" I asked Lacey.

She shrugged. "The same."

"Did the office survive my being out yesterday?" I asked.

"Just barely." Lacey smiled and leaned over the table. "Shaw is losing it."

"What else is new?"

"No, Allison, I mean it. He's becoming unpredictable. Yesterday, he and Sam Greely almost came to blows. Shaw finds fault with everything. He's always ticked off. You should have seen Sam

Greely. Shaw has been riding him lately, and I know he hates Shaw at this point.

"Do you think Shaw is worst?" I asked.

"Yes. Greely wants to quit."

I knew Sam Greely to be an excellent sports editor and had brought The Courier sports section from practically nonexistent to one of the most popular sections of the paper. My mind returned to the newspaper clipping I found in Blaire's room. I wanted to confront Shaw about his relationship with Blaire because I knew there was one. Why was I so sure, and was I only making trouble for myself? Why was I so sure? Because Shaw's personality changed as soon as my roommate disappeared and that other girl was found. I didn't believe it was a coincidence. I tried, but it didn't add up. The way Shaw was acting, something was eating him up inside. He wouldn't ask for help. The only trouble was I didn't know how deep our friendship went and if I could invade his privacy.

After lunch, the office was manageable. I contemplated approaching Shaw, but when I went into his office in the afternoon, his desk was cleared, and Lacey told me he had left for the day. I left an hour early myself, wanting to rest before the public meeting at the Rod and Gun Club meeting tonight.

At home, I nursed my elbow, deciding to let the air in. Maybe it would heal sooner. I napped for an hour, got my notebook and tape recorder out and made supper. I gave myself twenty minutes to get to the meeting. That's usually ten minutes before everything started, which allowed me to mingle. It's interesting to observe or overhear what people are saying at a meeting where the town fathers circulate to persuade or dissuade them from an issue. And, on a smaller scale, to socialize and keep in touch. It was no different tonight as I took my usual seat in the first row. People talk softly, others cough, clear their throats or do other things, and it's hard to hear what is being said. I wanted to be close to the Selectmen since they would make the final decision tonight. I also enjoyed reading their faces while the town folk made a point.

Where had my roommate been seated that night? Did she make the meeting? I know she started for the meeting. Who had she seen? Who had she talked to? And, what was the reason she disappeared?

Residents started trickling in. By seven thirty, the auditorium was full with people standing two deep in the back.

Selectmen Chairman George DiPesto opened the meeting, sounding his gavel three times before he got the room quiet.

"This public hearing is called to order. Residents and other interested parties, we are here tonight to vote on the request of the Rod and Gun Club, 545 Northern Road, Sandy Ridge, Maine, to obtain a permanent liquor license for their establishment."

A chorus of boos and cheers followed DiPesto's remarks. Geez, residents, especially guys, get into such a fervor over how accessible they can get their booze. It's going to be a long night, I thought.

The chairman struck his gavel. His face registered restrained anger.

"Now, I know this is a controversial issue, but I want everyone to conduct themselves in an orderly manner," said DiPesto. "Otherwise, the town's finest will show you the door." The chairman's eyes went to the many police around the room. He looked over at his colleagues for approval. They nodded.

I knew that all of the police had been called in for tonight's meeting because of the volatile feelings on both sides concerning the license. I saw Ted.

What a hunk, I thought. He was being super cop tonight, so he ignored me.

Great!

"I'm going to ask Burt Olson to speak first on behalf of the opposition to the license," said DiPesto. "Then, I want Bernie Edwards to speak on behalf of the Rod and Gun Club. Please be patient. Everyone will have a chance to speak. I will not allow this meeting to get out of control. Anyone wanting to say something, please raise your hand and wait to be recognized. I expect everyone to talk in a courteous tone, and there will be no obscenities." DiPesto told the audience again how they would be kicked out if they didn't follow the rules.

DiPesto took a handkerchief from his breast pocket and wiped his brow. He was at least fifty pounds overweight and had a ruddy complexion that now was beet red. Is any doctor in the house? The air smelled of tension, and the evening had just begun.

Olson came up to the front of the room when DiPesto called his name. I like Olson, but man, that guy can rattle on. Tonight, was no exception. I had heard his spiel anytime I ran into him. They were real issues: driving while intoxicated, speed bumps that selectmen promised but never put in on the street, and motorcycles roaring down the street late at night. It was a fact that there were four families on the street with young children from three to eight years old.

"The possibility of some child getting hurt or killed is just too risky," said Olson.

"Let the Rod and Gun Club move their club to an isolated spot in town. Where they are now is a health hazard to those who live on that street."

Olson was interrupted several times by people in the back. DiPesto shot them a warning look. They shut up temporarily but soon began talking to the people in the back row. Others joined in. DiPesto sounded his gavel, nodded to the police and the two were shown the exit. They didn't go willingly, and it took time for the crowd to settle down. Olsen talked louder and louder through the incident, wanting his points to be heard.

DiPesto regained order. Olson was still talking. DiPesto asked him to soften his voice. Without a beat, Olson proposed the gun club relocate to a spot further out of town.

"What happens to the present location?" asked a voice in the back of the auditorium. Olson suggested the town use the present location for a recreation hall for Sandy Ridge youths.

"The Recreation Department could keep softball, soccer and football equipment in there. There's land that could be made into a baseball, soccer or football field. And, how about putting computers in there and having courses for residents that could make the town some money."

The ideas met with a chorus of boos. Those people are only thinking of themselves, I thought. How about a senior center? The town didn't have one. They always talked an issue into the ground before anything happened, like the speed bumps that Olson never got for his street.

DiPesto asked Olson if he had anything else to say. The man shook his head and sat down.

It was Bernie Edward's turn to talk in favor of the permanent liquor license. He told the audience that his intentions were honorable. He was the present manager of the Rod and Gun Club.

"I am attempting to take the club and make it a money-making venture for the town. Industry is coming to Sandy Ridge at a rapid rate, and the town doesn't have any function halls to hold parties. We must keep up. Otherwise, we lose money that could benefit the town," said Edwards.

A voice I recognized as Sophie Blake yelled, "How can the town benefit from you guys drinking and acting disorderly?"

The club manager was not phased but instead pulled an easel over to the center of the room, went to the Selectman's table, took some blueprints and put them on the easel.

"Who the hell can see those?" yelled a voice.

With patience, Edwards continued. "Let me explain then. Everyone is welcome to come up after the meeting and view these plans. I'll be available after the meeting for questions. But right now, let me tell you about what the club hopes to accomplish."

The man was composed and described how the club would add another bar with several rooms being built that could open up to a larger room, with another bar being in the center, or for smaller parties, there would be partitions to block the room off.

The club manager said that if the club got a permanent liquor license, they would donate ten percent of each seminar or party to the town's recreation board to help build more ball fields for the youth of the town.

"I will be personally responsible that no one will leave the club intoxicated."

How the hell can he do that? I thought. Is anybody buying that?

A hand was raised in the middle row. "Bernie, you know you are not at the club all the time. It isn't possible to check on the state of sobriety of everyone that leaves the club."

Edwards said he has staff that will help him.

Olson's group booed over that.

Drunks checking on drunks, I thought. Edwards was being too idealistic about what could be an explosive situation. I imagined the fights that could ensue stopping someone from driving after having a few.

Once Edwards spoke, DiPesto encouraged residents to ask questions, and those involved in the issue answered them for about an hour.

It was getting late. At 11 p.m., DiPesto said he'd take two more questions. People were straining for more, but the selectman was firm. I had caught him yawning a couple of times. I didn't blame him.

"The Selectmen want what is best for the town. We want to be fair to all residents of the town and surrounding towns that will be using the Rod and Gun Club while being fair to the abutters of the club. For that reason, the selectmen will go into Executive Session. You are encouraged to wait if you like, but the hour is late. You might want to read about it in the newspaper tomorrow." He glanced over at me, smiling.

People streamed out of the meeting. Some die-hards stayed. I wandered over to Olson, got his ideas of how the meeting went, and I needed to clear up some details with Edwards. While waiting for Selectmen to get out of the Executive Session, I formulated the story I knew would be on the front page of tomorrow's edition.

When the town board goes into private session, it can be minutes or hours, many hours, before they come out. It's anyone's guess. After twenty minutes, I started pacing. I was tired. Someone was going out for coffee. I declined, not wanting caffeine to keep me up any longer than I knew I would be writing my story.

Forty minutes later, Selectmen came out. They took their seats at the front of the auditorium. DiPesto cleared his throat and looked at his fellow Selectmen before giving the remaining residents there his attention.

"The Selectmen have given the matter before the board tonight serious thought and discussion. We have voted unanimously to give the Rod and Gun Club a six-month temporary liquor license."

A chorus of cheers went up. DiPesto sounded his gavel.

"There will be none of that," he said firmly. "Bernie, if there are any infractions in that six months, your group will be brought before the Selectmen, and your license will be revoked. And it will be a long time before you get another one. Do you understand?"

Edwards was elated. He would have agreed to anything.

DiPesto continued. "Burt, I know the town has been delinquent on the subject of the speed bumps for your street. We have discussed this with the police, and speed bumps will be in place on your street by April 1."

It was not what Olson hoped the town fathers would say, but he took it as a generous gesture, one that was certainly due him after many requests.

I was tired, my elbow was throbbing, and I wanted nothing more than to get out of there, write up my story for tomorrow's edition and get into bed. But that wasn't to be yet.

Olson stood up. "Chairman DiPesto, let it be in the recorded minutes that I object to the vote of the Selectmen. I feel we have not discussed the matter thoroughly enough, and the temporary liquor license will be trouble for the town."

"Burt, we've heard how you feel. We can't talk this thing to death, and I won't. Selectmen, after much thought, have made a decision. The stenographer has made note of your comments that will become a matter of record," continued DiPesto. "The town board considers this a compromise, and rest assured, we will monitor the Rod and Gun Club during the next six months.

Olson shook his head in dismay. He and his contingent got up to leave. At the door, Olson took a parting shot. "You're going to be sorry." I rushed out the door to catch up with Olson.

"What did you mean by that?" Olson said he would talk to his attorney, who had been there earlier. He was going to get a petition up to have the liquor license issue put on the warrant for the Annual Town Meeting. "Tonight, was disappointing, but we haven't begun to fight," said Olson.

"If nothing else, you got Selectmen to approve the speed bumps for your street," I offered.

"I'm very appreciative that we'll have those installed," said Olson. "I hope it will not be too late."

I asked him what he meant by that.

Olson said the speed bumps take time. "Maybe they won't help. I hope nobody gets hurt or killed as a result of the decisions made tonight."

We parted. I went inside. The place had pretty much cleared out. I caught Edwards, who gave me a few good quotes for my story. He thanked Selectmen for their forward thinking.

My last input for the story was from DiPesto. Then, I went home, wrote up the story and sent it over to The Courier. Feeling good about having finished, I looked in the refrigerator for something good. Not finding anything, I took a shot of whiskey and went to bed.

Chapter 9

It's funny how when you get very little sleep and think you'll sleep 'til noon the next day, nature plays a trick on you, and you can't sleep at five a.m. I was wide awake. A half-hour later, I decided to get up. After showering, dressing and eating breakfast, I walked into the office at 7:30 a.m.

In the afternoon, I was caught up. It was then I noticed a light in Shaw's office. He was sitting at his desk but didn't appear to be working. Shaw looked up. He appeared to be disheveled and had one day's growth of beard. He looked confused. I went in.

"Did some crucial news story come in?" I asked. "It looks like you've been here all night."

"Since when are you keeping tabs on me?"

"Since you haven't been yourself." There's nothing subtle about me.

"You've noticed?"

I told him everyone at the newspaper had and offered to help should he want to talk to me.

My boss shrugged. "Thanks, but I've got to think this out for myself."

We sat there facing each other, both in our own thoughts. "You're in early," he observed.

"Couldn't sleep. Too charged up about the meeting last night." I looked over at Shaw. He could have cared less about what I said.

"You have a lot to catch up with, what with you being out the other day," he said.

"Don't worry, I finished everything." Shaw nodded. He wanted me to leave, but I didn't want to miss my chance to ask him why he had hired Blaire, or whoever she was, who obviously was not a newspaper reporter.

"Boss, does your problem have anything to do with my roommate who disappeared?"

If looks could kill, I'd be pushing up daisies right now.

"You better get to work before you get into trouble, little lady."

I couldn't back down now.

"She didn't have any newspaper experience, yet you hired her. And why, since I was working on the Rod and Gun Club issue, did you give it to her to cover? Also, I found a clipping of you taken at an awards banquet in New York. It was in my roommate's personal belongings."

Shaw wondered why that should concern me. "Who I hire and what I give them for assignments is not any of your business. You're just sore because she got the assignment."

"The hell I am, and who ended up doing it?"

Shaw rose and came towards me. His expression was dark as a rainy night. He leaned against his desk and looked straight at me.

"Girlie, be careful here. You might get into trouble with that mouth of yours." He told me if I had a problem with who he hired, he couldn't help me. He eyeballed me closer. I saw faint traces of acne scars from years ago. His eyes had red veins around the pupil.

"Now get this once and for all. I don't know anything about a newspaper clipping that girl may have had. You've been reading too many mysteries, Allison, or maybe you don't have enough to do. Watch yourself, or you may be out on your ear." My boss flipped my chair around. Dizzy, I reached for something to stop me. Was Shaw out of control? Would he actually hurt me? When I rose and started for the door, he started yelling obscenities at me. As grumpy as the guy was, I had never heard him swear with such force. Why didn't I know when to keep my mouth shut? Trembling, but never one to admit defeat, I said, "Boss, you need help with whatever is bothering you. If you don't want to talk to me, then someone else." I told him it wasn't a coincidence that my roommate disappeared, a girl was murdered, and his troubled state happened at the same time.

"Who is she to you?" I asked. "You'll feel a lot better if you talk about it."

Looking back, I chided myself for saying those things why I didn't run like hell out of that room. I had never seen Shaw like this before. For all I knew, he could be the murderer. I guess the adrenaline was flowing, and I couldn't help myself.

Shaw called me a "nosy bitch," that needed straightening out. "You could get hurt if you're not careful," he warned. He told me I was a lousy reporter, and he wanted me out of his newsroom right away. "As of now, you're fired," he yelled.

I stared at Shaw, not wanting to understand. "Get out of here. You're fired.

He swept his arm out and hit my elbow. I shrank back. Shaw was as tall as he was wide. Hurt, emotionally and physically, I ran out of my former boss's office, nearly colliding with the suburban editor, Howie Dunn, coming in with coffee and two glazed donuts for my boss, something Dunn did every morning.

"Everything OK in here?" Dunn stammered. He saw tears in my eyes and turned to Shaw.

Shaw yelled. "Everything's fine. Allison was just leaving for good, I hope. Anything I hate is a noisy dame."

I turned around, choked up, eyes blazing. "This noisy dame, as you call me, gave you headlines and increased circulation. See how it is without me, you jerk." Dunn looked like he wanted to be invisible. I pushed past Dunn and went to my desk. Sobbing, I was aware of people coming into work for the day, looking at me.

Dunn came over to me, "What the hell is going on with Shaw?" he asked. I couldn't answer.

"He doesn't mean what he said," said Dunn, trying to placate me. "Here, have a donut." Dunn reached over to his desk, got the box and put it in front of me. What was I to do? I took two: one chocolate and one glazed. Chopping on the chocolate, Dunn told me Shaw hadn't been himself lately.

No kidding!

"Diane and I have noticed it ourselves," continued Dunn. He was married to Shaw's sister. He touched my hand. "I'm sorry." I finished the last of the chocolate donuts. With the glazed in my hand, I asked for another. Dunn was happy to retreat to his desk. I put the glazed back and tried the chocolate crème next. Finished, I ran to the bathroom, barely making it. A girl from the newsroom made a hasty retreat. Geez, those donuts tasted delicious going down.

I didn't want to go back into the newsroom. Instead, I went down to my car, parked in the garage, got in and started bawling. I lost track of time, but when I heard car doors around me slamming and people talking, I attempted to regain my composure and left.

It had been a bad couple of days. My elbow throbbed. I just got fired. If the car didn't start......But luck was with me, and my car started, and I drove home. On the way, I started crying again and pulled over to the side of the road. How could Shaw talk to me like that? I was the best reporter at The Courier, and he knew it. News stories hit The Courier before any of the other newspapers in the area because of my quick action and ability to smell a story that was of interest to the town. Shaw would be eating crow in the morning.

CHAPTER 10

Even Muffy couldn't stand me and wanted to go out when I got home. Having nothing else to do, I turned on one of those dirty talk shows that aired in the morning hours. Who watches those anyway? Today, there was a gay guy with two straight wives or girlfriends. The other woman's husband, a gay guy too, was in the wings scheduled to come out as soon as the one guy on stage admitted to his wife of twenty years that he was gay.

I laid down on the couch and took a nap. The show didn't hold my interest. What can I say? When I woke up, a soap opera was on. I shut the TV off and decided to go to the local burger joint. There's nothing like a cheeseburger deluxe and fries to soothe one's nerves.

The afternoon went slowly. I watched a video, cooked something light for supper since I had heartburn from lunch, and took a good book to bed with me.

The next couple of days went by without a word from Shaw. The third day, I knew he wouldn't call. While I waited, I was eating a lot of junk food and the healthy stuff in the refrigerator went bad, so I threw it out. I became interested in dirty talk shows and started rooting for the people who got into fights. I became an avid fan of one of the soap operas and set my alarm so I wouldn't miss the beginning. I wore the same T-shirt and jeans day after day. Some days, I stayed in my pajamas and bathrobe. What the hell? I wasn't going anywhere. I ordered Chinese food and fast food so much the guy at the burger joint asked me out.

Days moved into weeks. Weeks into months. My money dwindled, and I got scared.

Lacey had been calling every day, asking how things were. Pretty soon, she stopped. I didn't have anything to report and cried often on the telephone. I kept asking how the office was and how Shaw was getting along without me. One day, Lacey snapped at me.

"Allison, get a grip. Shaw's not going to ask you to come back. Don't ask about him anymore. He's an idiot. It's his loss, and get on with your life. Try and get a job Didn't you say the daily in Portland is hiring?"

After that, she didn't call. That was OK with me. I don't need anybody. Naps and tears were a large part of my days.

One Saturday morning, I went down to the foyer to get my mail, leaving my door ajar. I took my mailbox key, that was on a separate key ring. Why had I done that? I vaguely remember giving it to a neighbor when going on vacation for a week. Geez, that was a while ago. After I got my mail, I'd get the key and put them all on the same key ring.

The young couple upstairs were down in the lobby getting their mail after coming in from outside. They were honeymooners. I used to think it was cute the way they stared at each other like there was no other person in the world. But today, it bugged the hell out of me.

I said hi. They returned my greeting, but I sensed their disapproval. It was eleven o'clock in the morning, and I was in my blue chenille bathrobe. I wanted to tell them that I had the flu. I wanted to tell them I had been fired. But they had that look like they wanted to jump each other's bones and needed to rush upstairs. Just then, the good-looking guy from across the way came in the front door. I smiled, trying to smooth my hair down. He brushed past me, not giving me a look.

I got my mail. Bills, what else? I tried to grab the foyer door before the dream guy went in, but I was busy smoothing my hair down as if he cared. The door shut before me. The dream guy ran up the stairs before I realized what happened. Shoot, what do I do now?

I pressed the intercom, but no one answered to buzz me in. Isn't anyone home on a Saturday morning? Ten minutes went by. I decided to go out and sit on the front stairs and wait until someone came along. It was a mild October day, with sun and no clouds in sight. The sky was a light blue, and it was peaceful there in the quiet, with only the birds chirping. I let the sun wrap its warmth around me. The trees were slowly turning color, but few leaves had toppled to the ground yet to become enmeshed with the earth.

One of the things I liked about living here was the country setting and the maintenance people kept the grass green and professionally mowed. Geraniums and petunias dotted the walkway amongst manicured shrubs.

A half hour went by. I need to find one of the maintenance men, I thought. They have extra keys. A breeze suddenly came up. My bathrobe opened up, exposing me in my underwear, but nobody, thank goodness, was around.

I went into other units and tried their intercoms. Geez, the complex was deserted. I walked around the buildings. The air was growing cooler. A breeze became wind. I kept telling myself to stay calm. Nearly exhausted, I found George, one of the men who took care of the units.

"I'm so glad to see you," I said.

George looked confused as he saw me in my bathrobe. I quickly told him I had gotten locked out of my apartment and needed him to let me in.

"Y,y,y, y,y, you don't have your keys?" George stuttered. He does that when he gets nervous, I had noticed.

"It's a long story, George. I went down for my mail, and someone came in and shut the door after them before I could grab the door."

"Y,y,y, you don't have your mail key with your door keys?"

"I will after this if I get into my condo," I said. "You see, I lost my mail key, and someone lent me theirs until I got a duplicate, and I never put the new mail key with my other keys."

George looked more confused. I knew that the more I explained, the worse his confusion would get. "Can you just let me into my condo?"

The maintenance man hesitated. "Thank you for helping me. I know you're busy." George kept looking at my bathrobe, which opened up continually, with me repeatedly holding the robe closed in despair. We both started walking toward my place.

"You see, George, I had the flu, and today was my first venture outside."

I was relieved when we got to my unit, and he unlocked the foyer door. Funny, I had never noticed a twinkle in George's eyes before, but there was one now.

"Oh George, thank you, thank you. You have saved the day."

George lingered. "A, A, A, Allison, you've been living here quite some time, haven't you?"

"Three years." He got to the point quickly.

"W,w,w,w, would you like to go out with me sometime?"

I looked at him, unable to find my voice. George was tall, lanky, fortyish. I guessed him to be. He knew his stuff around gardening but didn't appear to be too savvy if you know what I mean. He wore his gray hair long in a ponytail, his eyebrows running together. And today, I noticed a bad case of halitosis.

He looked at me with great expectations.

"Gee, sometime maybe we can go out for a pizza," I said and ran up the stairs. I looked behind me to see if he was following me, but he wasn't. He was in the foyer with a smile on his face.

I rushed into my condo and slammed the door. I ran into my bedroom and looked in the mirror. My hair was tossed by the wind, I noticed a couple of gaping holes in my bathrobe, and I probably had bad breath as well because I hadn't brushed that morning. George probably thought we were just right for each other.

Now I'll have to move or hibernate because George will not leave me alone until I go out with him. The bathrobe had fit me once. What happened? I went into the bathroom and weighed myself. It went to new heights. I sat on the toilet and cried.

CHAPTER 11

After a good cry, which was the norm lately, I spent the afternoon showering, washing my hair, shaving my legs, underarms, and doing my nails. Then I got dressed, not in sweatshirts and jeans I had been wearing, but in something presentable. At least, I thought it was. I fixed supper and thought of going out, but instead looked in the newspaper and on the Internet for reporter jobs in Portland. There were three, so I felt hopeful. I copied the addresses and phone numbers and went to bed telling myself that I would send my resume to each job opportunity the next day, which I did. I was on track again.

Ted hadn't called since our fateful night in the ER. Perhaps he was waiting for my elbow to clear up before we had another clandestine night of possible sex. Ted was always on my mind, but also Blaire, or the girl that called herself Blaire, who had been my roommate only for a short while. Where was she? I knew I couldn't walk away from finding her. Was she alright? Why had she disappeared, and what was her real name?

What bothered me was that I knew my former roommate didn't have any journalist experience, but how was I going to prove that? The more I thought about that, though, I knew it was just my pride. The Rod and Gun issue before the town had been my story, and it still burned me that Shaw had given it to my roommate when I had done all the prior work.

An idea came to me one evening while watching TV. I needed to find a copy of Blaire's resume. That way, I could prove she didn't have any journalist knowledge. But I would need help. I called Lacey.

"Are you still my friend," I asked.

"We never stopped being friends, Allison. I just hated seeing you down on yourself so much," said Lacey.

We talked a bit, catching up on things. I told her I had sent resumes out and was using the Internet to pursue writing opportunities. I didn't ask about Shaw or how the newspaper was doing. After about ten minutes, Lacey said she'd call again but had to get off. Faithfully, Lacey called every day.

I needed a favor from Lacey, but I didn't want her to get into trouble and get fired like me. I toyed with asking her every time she called but chickened out until the desire to do the deed got the best of me, and I came out with it.

"Lacey, I need a favor."

She hesitated, wondering what was coming.

"I need a copy of Blaire's resume."

Silence.

"Lacey, hear me out. If you can get a copy of her resume from Shaw's office, maybe there's something in there that will help me track her down. Maybe she listed references. If she did, I can track them down. I also want to see if she has any friends around here."

"Why would she know anybody here?" asked my friend.

"Then who helped my former roommate move her things out of my condo? She must have had some help. This appears to be a mystery with no solution, but we both know there's a reason for everything."

"Allison, you've got to forget your former roommate."

I told Lacey I couldn't. "I need to know what happened to her. Please, Lacey," I begged. "Please do this, and you won't hear any more from me about her."

"Yeah, sure."

"I mean it, Lacey. You are the only one who can help me. Either that or I'll have to do it myself."

Lacey told me she didn't want to hear how I would do that. My friend sighed. "OK, what do you want me to do?"

Lacey and I knew that if there was a resume, it would be in Shaw's office in the personnel files. Lacey would try to find it, make a copy and give it to me. Only Lacey could determine when the time was right to do the search for the resume.

I didn't hear from Lacey for several days, but on a Friday, she called to tell me Shaw was out of town.

"Where did he go?"

"Who cares," Lacey said excitedly. "Let's see, it's ten o'clock now. I'll get into his office with the pretense of filing and look for the resume. When I find it, I'll make a copy and give it to you at lunch. Are you still meeting me?"

"Great," I said. "Let's go to the diner that we've been going to. Around noon?"

Elated, I busied myself around the condo, but the time passed agonizingly slow. At eleven thirty, I left for the place that was fast becoming our place. When Lacey came through the door, she wasn't smiling. We didn't say anything until the waitress brought us coffee.

"Well?" I asked.

"Allison, this isn't a good idea. You know that girl didn't have any newspaper experience. Why do you need any further proof?"

Lacey thought about what she had just said, smiled and looked at me.

"You want proof to show Shaw. It's still all about Shaw. Screw him and get on with your life, for God's sake."

I wanted to keep my cool. I needed Lacey as a friend, but she was also in a position to find the information I desired. "Did you look for Blaire's resume at all?"

"Why do you still call her Blaire? Blaire is the girl that was murdered."

"I don't know what else to call her?" I said. "Shall I call her 'Blaire impersonator'?"

Lacey shrugged her shoulders. "OK, as long as we know it's really your former roommate we're talking about."

"Well?" "Yes, I looked, but Blaire's resume was not there. Everyone else was in the personnel folder, but not hers.

"That tells me there wasn't a resume."

Lacey disagreed, saying maybe Shaw took it out for some reason. I asked her, "Why would my former boss do that?"

"In case the cops come to look in the files."

Lacey was confusing me. My friend noticed and explained, "If Shaw killed the girl found in the woods, he would want to destroy everything that connected him to her, wouldn't he?"

My friend had a point there. "You just don't want to think Shaw's a murderer," she told me.

I agreed. "He's got problems, but murder is going a bit too far." I shivered. Images of the last time in Shaw's office came to mind. Shaw had been ugly when he twirled me around in that chair. The look he gave me then as he fired me made me cringe now. Where does that leave me? I thought.

Sensing my disappointment, Lacey tried to comfort me. "That's why I didn't want to tell you. I thought maybe if I said I'd changed my mind about looking for the resume, you would let it go."

"You know me better than that," I said.

We laughed. The waitress came over for the second time. We quickly screened the menu and ordered.

Halfway through our salads, Lacey suggested I come back with her to the office and say hi to everyone since Shaw was not there.

"You have to clean out your desk anyway, and the gang would love to see you."

That sounded good to me. And it was. The gang wanted to know how I was doing; did I get another newspaper job? I told them I was still looking. The truth was I was waiting for Shaw to apologize, and since he hadn't, my heart was broken. Of course, I couldn't tell my friends that. I was able to catch up with my fellow workers, and we laughed and joked. My spirits soared, seeing how happy everyone was to see me. When my friends told me how much they missed my corny jokes, I realized how much I missed them as well.

Lacey got me an empty box from the back room, and I proceeded to clean out my desk. I patted the top of my desk as if it was a rare antique. How long had I sat in this chair, breaking top stories, being at the pulse of murders, elections and other life-changing situations? I sighed.

Rose, from the computer next to mine, heard and looked over.

"We all miss you, Allison."

I smiled weakly and said, "Thanks. How has it been around here without me?"

Rose shrugged. "There hasn't been a lot of work since…." Rose looked at me embarrassed.

"Since Shaw fired me. It's OK, Rose, to say it."

There was an awkward silence. "What are you working on?" I asked.

"The damn Rod and Gun Club issue won't die. Colin Reed now says that if the club can't get a permanent liquor license, he's going to withdraw his offer to give the club the land. Sounds like he may have another buyer."

"Who?"

"He won't say, but the club's board is nervous. All their plans for enlarging the club could go sour without Colin Reed." Rose looked at her work on the computer screen.

"I'll let you get back to work." Leaving my desk contents box on my desk, I went into Shaw's office. Lacey followed me in. "Now, what are you going to do?"

"Might as well have a look while I'm here."

My friend told me I drove her crazy with my antics.

"Did anyone see you come in here?"

"No, they're all working." I smiled, walking to the file cabinet where I knew Shaw kept the personnel folders. Lacey started to object.

I held up my hand to stop Lacey in her tracks. "Stand at the door, then, if you want, and warn me if someone comes."

A search proved Lacey was right. There wasn't anything in the files about my missing roommate. "Damn."

"C'mon, I'll walk you to your car."

"What, you want to get rid of me so soon?"

Lacey shook her head. I retrieved the box from my desk, said goodbye to everyone and promised to come back to visit. Lacey and I walked out silently. At my car, Lacey asked me what scheme I was cooking up in my mind.

"Why would you say that?" I asked.

"Because I know that look you're wearing right now," said Lacey.

Damn, I didn't give my friend that much credit. "There's another place Shaw could have put Blaire's resume."

"NO, NO," screamed Lacey. "One minute, you say there was no resume. Today you're looking in the personnel files, didn't find it there, now you thought of another place. What you should be saying is, 'the hell with Shaw, the hell with Blaire,' now you're back to square one again."

"You don't have to come with me. I still have my key, but not for long, so I'll have to go tonight."

"Are you crazy?"

"There are rumors to that effect."

"I don't want to talk to you about this anymore. I'm out."

I told her that was fine with me, that I appreciated her help so far, and that was that. Trying to change the conversation to more benign subjects, I asked Lacey whether they had filled my position.

"I saw my job advertised in the newspaper."

"No. Shaw's been interviewing but hasn't decided on anyone. I didn't mention it because……. well, you know."

"Yeah." We were at my car. Lacey hugged me. My mood had changed, and I felt lousy again. With a promise to get together soon, I put the box from my old desk into my backseat, got in the car, waved to Lacey, and I was off for home.

I'd been so happy earlier, talking to my friends, joking. They assumed I would have a job. Of course, one has to feel good enough about themselves to send out resumes. I hadn't even updated mine, so how could I send it out?

I was humiliated that Lacey paid for lunch, but she insisted and even went to our waitress to pay her. My friend said she "wanted to treat me." But I knew her financial situation was as bleak as mine, so I promised to pay the next time.

Once home, I let Muffy out and fixed myself a drink. It would help the throbbing in my elbow. I took some chocolate bars and put them in my coat pocket, just in case I got hungry as I burgled Shaw's office that night. After which, I went in to take a nap.

How could Shaw hire anyone to take my place at The Courier? Seeing my friends today made me realize how much I missed my job and my colleagues. My black mood remained. Dinner was quiet as I pondered my mission for the evening.

That afternoon, I found Shaw's middle desk drawer locked. When there was no resume for Blaire in the personnel folders, I realized it could be in that middle drawer. I would need a screwdriver to get into the drawer. I quickly found one. I chose a couple of other sharp tools in case the screwdriver didn't work. This would be my last chance, and I needed to find what I wanted as I opened Shaw's desk. I put my tools in my purse and decided to take another nap. I set the alarm for one-thirty in the morning but was awakened by a phone call around eleven.

"Did I wake you up?" asked Lacey.

"What do you think? I'm nervous as hell. How can I sleep? Why aren't you in bed? Is something wrong with your father?"

Lacey had trouble spitting it out. Finally, she said it so fast that I wasn't sure I heard her correctly.

"Did you say you're going with me?" Earlier I had told Lacey I was going to use my key to get into the newspaper office, and Shaw's locked desk drawer. I had to for my own satisfaction. My friend, of course, said she wasn't going to come with me.

"Yes," said Lacey. She told me she didn't like what I was doing, but she didn't want me to do it alone. We decided to meet in front of The Courier at two a.m. The night crew left at that time, and we would have several hours before the morning crew came in at six a.m.

"Get some sleep and wear dark clothes," was my sign-off.

Chapter 12

I was jumpy about what I was going to do. But at 1:45 a.m., when my bedroom alarm went off, I was ready. I was in dark clothes, a hooded shirt to put over my head should anyone detect me. I put new batteries in two flashlights; one for Lacey, in case she forgot hers.

Sandy Ridge was quiet, even scary, in the early morning hours. Oh, yes, there was the occasional car, but the town was taking a siesta. Exactly at two p.m., I pulled up to the newspaper office. Lacey wasn't there. I waited ten minutes and then decided to go in. My friend probably decided against our adventure. I got out of the car and walked to the front door. It was then Lacey drove up.

"I overslept," she apologized. I was glad to see her.

"Here's a flashlight, in case you forgot one." My friend grabbed it and tried it. The light highlighted the door. It was grimy with a lot of crap I didn't want to venture into thinking about, with choice words one doesn't say in public sprawled in red paint. I never noticed because I always parked in the underground garage and walked into the newspaper office from there.

I unlocked the door. It squeaked. Lacey jumped, scared the hell out of me.

"Sorry."

We walked up the ten stairs to the foyer of The Courier, passed the receptionist's desk, and entered the darkened newsroom. I stood, attempting to get used to the darkness. Streetlights from the outside fell eerily on the vacant desks. Shaw's office was up and to the left. I went in.

"Lacey, you stand outside here in case we're interrupted. You can warn me." My friend looked ill at that prospect.

Once inside, I went to Shaw's desk. I pried open the middle drawer with the tools I had brought. Nothing. I opened the other drawers on the desk. Lacey was right. My former roommate's resume was not there.

Shaw had papers on top of a bookcase. Nothing.

Damn. I stood in Shaw's office, flashlight down, trying to figure out what to do next. I went to his secretary's desk outside the door. Perhaps my ex-boss had given my roomie's data to his secretary to keep in case I came snooping.

God, Allison, do you hear yourself? Shaw doesn't give a damn about you, you should write him off and get on with your own life. Yeah. Sure! Where else could the resume be? I was out of ideas and sat on a chair to think.

Suddenly, I was broken out of my thoughts by a booming voice and a flashlight in my face.

"Stay right where you are, and don't move. This is the security police, and you are under arrest."

I dropped my flashlight as if zapped by an electric shock. "I'm not armed," I yelled.

"Don't move," the tall figure in front of me repeated. I wished he wouldn't keep saying that since I wasn't going anywhere. I wanted to crawl into the woodwork and desperately needed to pee all of a sudden. Oh, what an embarrassment if I had an accident.

The guard backed up and switched on the light. The illumination blinded both of us for a second. Then, we assessed each other.

"Allison, what the hell are you doing here?"

"You wouldn't believe it if I told you. Can I sit down?" He nodded. Once seated, I put my head between my legs in case I vomited.

"Don't try anything funny.".

I'd known Joe, the security guard, for three years. He was a cheery, middle-aged man with deep brown eyes who loved to talk about his grandchildren. I had never heard him shout, and it was very unnerving. But, as I looked at him now, Joe's right hand, where he held his gun, had a slight tremor, and his Adam's apple was prominent. I heard police sirens in the distance.

"Oh, Joe, did you have to call the cops?" I asked.

"You did break in, Allison."

As we both listened, the police sirens got closer and soon were very loud.

Then doors were slamming, and what sounded like a stampede of horses were coming up the stairs. They opened the door with such force I shrank back. They stopped short upon seeing just Joe and I. Joe went over to the cops with bullet proof vests and explained how he found me. Then I saw Ted. His mouth fell open upon seeing me.

"What the hell is going on here?" he asked. I tried to speak, but nothing came out.

"Put away the guns, fellows," Ted said. "She's dangerous only to herself."

He came over to me. "What the hell are you up to?" he yelled. I told him how I was looking for my roommate's resume.

"Did you find it?"

"No. If there was one, Shaw would have destroyed it."

"Allison, if I hadn't been here, you would be in a lot more trouble than you are. Why did you try to find this resume in the middle of the night?"

I explained how Lacey had tried to find it earlier in the day but couldn't, so I still had a key and knew Shaw's middle drawer was locked. "I thought this was the only way to find what I wanted."

"But it isn't here, is it?"

Ted told me that I would have to accompany him down to the police station.

"Allison, what you did tonight was crazy. Joe could have shot you. You're losing it because that resume is important only in your mind. You've got to stop this."

Hall liked me, I knew, so I was hoping I wouldn't get into that much trouble.

Technically, I wasn't breaking in. I started thinking about what I would tell Hall.

Ted turned his back to me and told a fellow officer to cuff me.

"You don't have to do that," I scoffed.

"Read this young lady her rights," he commanded.

I hoped my wanting to kill Ted registered on my face. The cuffs were tight, and the rookie cop was rough with me.

Halfway out the door, I remembered Lacey. I stopped short.

"What now?" asked Ted.

"I forgot about my friend Lacey. Maybe she went home when she heard you coming, but maybe she's scared. I don't want to leave her."

"Call her and tell her it's OK to come out. I won't cuff her because I know you probably conned her into going with you." said Ted.

I called out Lacey's name and told her I was leaving with Ted, and I didn't want to leave her.

She yelled back, so I was glad she was still here. Actually, Lacey had been at her desk the whole time, just waiting for me to tell her I was done. I told her she wasn't in trouble. When Lacey joined us, Ted told her to pick her friends more carefully, or she might get into real trouble.

We didn't talk as the cops led us to the police cruiser, and Lacey said nothing as we traveled to the station. I stole a glance at her as we traveled to the station but couldn't read her expression. I just knew I had lost a friend.

Chapter 13

The drive to the police station seemed endless, and with every bump, the handcuffs dug deeper into my wrists. Lacey continued her silent treatment, and I didn't know what to do about that. When we got to the station, Ted asked if we wanted coffee, and we nodded in the affirmative. I got the directions to the bathroom and quickly took care of that. The coffee tasted good, and we waited. Ted took a position behind his desk until a red light indicated the chief would see us now.

Hall was surprised to see me enter with Ted, then saw Lacey, an unfamiliar face.

"Look who I found in the early morning hours breaking into The Courier," Ted smirked.

"Who's she?" asked Hall, indicating Lacey.

I introduced Lacey.

The chief sat back in his chair. "OK, Allison, tell me why you were at the newspaper in the middle of the night." His tone indicated I'd better have a great story.

I told him that since I had a key, I wanted to look for my roommate's resume.

"In the middle of the night? This is police business. How dare you take things into your own hands."

"I was trying to help since nothing seems to be happening with finding my roommate, Blaire, or whatever her name is."

"How do you know what's being done," the chief's tone went up an octave. "Do the police confer with you every time there's a lead? Do you think we ought to?"

I better try another tactic. "Look, chief, it was a stupid thing to do. I'm really sorry."

"And, what about you," Hall turned to Lacey.

"I told her I didn't want to do it, but she was going to anyway, so I figured maybe I could keep her from doing something she'd be sorry for. You know Allison can talk you into anything."

Thanks, Lacey, for your support.

Hall told my supposed friend that she should find others to hang out with because if she stayed with me, she might get more than she bargained for. Then he turned to me and asked what I thought had happened to Blaire's resume.

I wanted to tell him I didn't think there was a resume or that Shaw had thrown it away when I was questioning him about my former roommate's ability, but I didn't.

"I don't know," was my response.

Hall studied my face. "Sure, you do." He came closer.

"Allison, I'm going to have to call Shaw about your fiasco tonight. And I understand you still have your keys, so give them to me now."

Hall went back to his desk, perused his Rolodex and dialed. Was it too much to ask that Shaw not be home? Hall turned his back to me when Shaw came on the line, so I wasn't able to hear.

"Do you want more coffee?" asked Ted. Lacey said yes, but I declined. I wasn't sure how long we'd be here, and I didn't want to have to go to the bathroom again. Geez, didn't they have a cleaning lady to come in and tidy up?

Once again, Lacey was quiet. I looked over at her. She had sold me down the river to Hall, not justifying what I did at all. I truly had lost a friend with my scheme tonight, or was it last night since it was early the next day? I looked over at my friend. Her eyes were closing, and her face appeared ashen, or maybe that was the light in the police station.

"I'm sorry I got you into this," I said.

She gave me a smile. "Years from now, we'll laugh about this."

I wasn't too sure about that, but I was glad she was talking to me. Hall was talking to Shaw for a long time. I wonder what they were saying and how it affected me.

While we were waiting, Ted came in, pulled a chair over to me and asked me what I thought I was doing tonight, breaking into the newspaper.

"I already told you what I was doing," I said impatiently. "I was trying to find my former roommate's resume. Shaw had been acting so strange since she arrived in town and got the job at the newspaper.

"She told me she hoped to learn the writing business from me. I just know she didn't have any experience. Why, then, would Shaw hire her? And then, when that girl was murdered, Shaw completely lost it, yelling at everybody. There was something bothering him for sure. And when I tried to find out, he fired me. I figured that if I could find her resume, there might be references that I could consult to find her."

"Your former roommate could have killed that girl we found murdered. What do you think she would do to you if you got in her way?"

I then told Ted about the newspaper clipping I found in the girl's personal things. "She had something on Shaw."

"But you said Shaw denied it," said Ted. "Did you tell Hall about the clipping?

"No."

"Of course not. Hall should know about it because someone, probably her, came back and took her things, and she found the clipping in your room and took it."

"Yes, she did."

Ted urged me to tell Hall as soon as he got off the phone with Shaw. I shrugged. "Allison, I think you're the craziest dame I ever knew." He wrung his fingers through his hair, started to say something, but decided against it, and walked away.

It was another five minutes before Hall turned to face us again. Lacey appeared to be sleeping. Was she? How could anyone do that at a time like this?

"Allison, why didn't you tell me Shaw fired you?"

"The man freaked out when I started to ask questions about the girl he hired at the newspaper that I felt didn't know the first thing about journalism."

Hall came closer. "What does Shaw have to do with your former roommate?"

"Tell him about the clipping," urged Ted.

I told the chief about finding the newspaper clipping with my roomie and Shaw in an awards picture taken at a fancy hotel in New York where the owners of The Courier have their main headquarters. "Chief, when she came back and took all her things, she found the clipping I had put in my dressing table for safekeeping and took it.

"I believe she came to Sandy Ridge to find Shaw. The newspaper clipping is ten years old. Why would anyone carry a newspaper clipping around with them unless it had some meaning? I know that Shaw's personality changed for the worse after that girl came and was hired by him at the newspaper, and when the girl was found murdered in the woods that had the same name as my roommate, he was a tyrant and very irritable."

"Where does this leave us?" Hall asked. He cleared his throat. "Well, for now, stay away from Shaw. He said he would prosecute if you don't leave him alone. He's talking about getting a restraining order."

I couldn't believe Shaw would do that. It only showed me that Shaw was hiding something. I said that much to Hall. "Don't you think it strange that Shaw would have such a reaction if everything was completely innocent?"

"Leave it alone," said Ted.

Who asked him?

I ignored Ted's comments as I wished Hall to do, but I did want the chief to take seriously what I had told him.

"She and whoever my former roommate is came to town to find Shaw. Maybe she was blackmailing him about something."

Hall told me the clipping was food for thought. "But murder is not something you fool around with. Have you told me everything you know that would have a bearing on this case?"

"Yes," I answered.

Hall threw me a skeptical look. "What now?" Hall asked.

"I look for another job. I doubt whether Shaw will give me a reference, so it might be hard. What about Lacey and I being arrested tonight?"

"Your friend doesn't appear to be concerned," smiled Hall, looking at Lacey. I glanced over at my friend. Her eyes were closed, and her mouth was slightly open. Her peaceful countenance made me envious. Yet, in the back of my mind, I wondered if she was really sleeping, but why would she pretend?

"Wake your friend and get out of here," said the chief. I smiled, and he said he'd talk to Shaw and persuade him not to prosecute. "But listen, stay away from Shaw and this case and let us handle the police work or next time, I won't be as lenient."

I thanked him and smiled.

"You have a nice smile. Don't let anything happen to it."

"Chief, that's such an ominous remark."

"This is serious business, Allison. If your former roommate killed that woman, she will kill again."

"That's what Ted said."

Hall nodded.

"Will you ask Shaw about the resume?"

He sighed. "Don't push it, Allison. Haven't you learned anything from tonight?"

I walked over to Lacey, putting my hand on her shoulder when she opened her eyes. She didn't look sleepy at all. Had she been pretending? Who would do that?

She looked at me questioningly. "C'mon, Lacey, I can tell you all about it over breakfast."

CHAPTER 14

Lacey pleaded a headache. She then told me her father had fallen earlier in the evening, and Lacey had taken him to the Emergency Room before she met me.

"Actually, I got back to the house just before I planned to meet you," she explained. I made sure he was all right. He was snoring when I left the house."

"I wish you had called me because you didn't have to come with me. I would have understood."

My cohort didn't answer but told me she was going to call in sick that day. I personally looked forward to sleeping the day away. We parted in the parking lot, and I drove home slowly, not wanting to see another cop for a while.

Muffy was glad to see me. I tore off my clothes and jumped into bed. I vowed to stay there forever. Forever came with a telephone call at four that afternoon. It was Mother.

"I haven't heard from you this week," she said. "Is everything OK?" Mother dripped with solicitousness. What did she want?

She wanted me to come over that evening for dinner. Have you ever had people ask you something, and for some unknown reason, you say yes? Well, that's exactly what I did. I agreed the first time she asked me. Don't ask me why. She didn't have to argue or cajole or anything.

"We'll have dinner at seven. Come around six thirty, if you can," she said.

I wondered what that was all about. I hung up and looked at the clock. It was four-thirty. In a couple of hours, I would know. I jumped into the shower, got some coffee and dressed.

Mother hadn't said what she was serving, so I made a salad to take with me. Ronnie liked sauces and gravies and fancy ingredients, so if that was the route Mother was going, at least I could have the salad.

I left my place at 6:25 p.m. It was only ten minutes to Mother's house. She hadn't told me Joan and Doug were joining us, but their car was in front when I drove up.

My nephew Timmy greeted me at the door, his impish grin wide, his butterscotch, curly hair newly cut. "Aunt Allie, Aunt Allie," he yelled. I scooped him up in my arms.

"Stop, stop," he giggled, loving every minute of my kissing him.

"I can't stop," I said, tickling him.

Mother stood by for a few minutes. "OK, kids, can I have some of the action?"

I stared at her. Mother had never been demonstrative with me. Nevertheless, she came over and gave me a hug. Something was definitely up.

I went into the living room and greeted Joan and Doug. My sister had a top on that matched her blue eyes. Doug towered over her, always having a hug for his sister-in-law. He was a gentle yet highly intelligent guy, a healthy contrast to my sister, who could be a type A personality like myself. Ronnie came over. "Where's my hug?" he asked.

"Fresh out," I said, sidestepping him and moving towards my sister, our eyes meeting in sisterly understanding. Mother thought my response to her boyfriend was amusing.

"Ronnie likes to get the best of my serious daughter. Allison, you have to lighten up," she told me. "Ronnie doesn't bite." I shrugged.

"Isn't it great to have the family together," my Mother gushed. I took it as a rhetorical question and didn't reply.

Mother asked Ronnie to get the hors d'oeuvres. He went into the kitchen and returned with yummy-smelling bite-size cheese puffs. I took one because I didn't want Mother to comment on my not taking one and call attention to my weight, as she often did.

Soon, everyone was relaxing, and Mother returned to the kitchen to continue dinner preparations. I poked my head in and asked if I could help. She told me I could mash the potatoes. She told me with a lilt in her voice. My mother thought we were the Brady Bunch, more like Modern Family.

Joan came out with me and asked how she could help. Mother said to drain vegetables and put them on the table. I did my assigned job, found a dish, put my contribution in it and put it on the table. My mother told me I didn't have to bring the salad. I told her I knew that but didn't want to come empty-handed.

"Everything looks delicious," piped Joan as everyone sat down. I agreed. It was quite a feast. The bomb, whatever it was, must be big. Mother had all the foods she knew Joan and I loved. She was being very sweet. I grabbed Joan aside in the dining room. "What gives?"

"Eat a hearty meal. She wants to talk to us both after dinner."

Actually, the dinner was quite festive. Timmy wanted to sit next to my mother. She adored him and vice versa. I would like to think Mother knew she had screwed up with Joan and I and was trying to make up for it with Timmy. Plus, she was older. I'd like to think wisdom came to Mother with age, although the jury was still out.

Mother helped Timmy with his servings, mostly mashed potatoes, his favorite. She persuaded him to leave some for others. I sat next to my sister and Doug. Ronnie sat at the head of the table, as always. I wasn't going to tell Mother about my being fired, so I hoped she wouldn't ask about my job. I figured I'd wait until I got another job and then tell her I left since I wanted to advance myself. I did want to tell Joan as soon as we could be alone.

Talk around the dinner table centered on what good table manners Timmy had and what a good boy he was. We all adored Timmy, even Ronnie. He had grown children that he had never seen from a first marriage. He married upon his high school graduation. His girlfriend was sixteen, more than likely, pregnant. It lasted ten years. My thought was he probably was a deadbeat dad, maybe on a police flier somewhere as owing thousands of dollars for child support.

Dinner was cordial, and after everyone ate, I volunteered to bring the dessert in from the kitchen, which I did. Mother had heated the apple pie, and it looked delicious. I put it in front of my mother, who liked to cut and pass the pie around. She gave Doug and Ronnie a bigger piece and passed it to them first. They took it with acknowledgment and started eating. Mother passed Joan a slice. I shook my head and took out my apple, which was in my pocket. Mother cut herself a piece. I bit into my apple with a vengeance.

"Mother, this pie is delicious," said Joan. She nodded, finished hers and took another piece. Joan pleaded, being stuffed. Both of us brought the dishes to the kitchen, ran the dishwasher, and cleared the counters.

Everyone complimented Mother on the food. She gushed again and told me that Ronnie had cooked the turkey. I noticed then that Ronnie was holding my Mother's hand.

Doug asked Ronnie how the search for land to build the health club was coming. Ronnie hesitated and looked at my Mother.

"Let's not talk business around the dinner table," my Mother said. Her saccharin tone was nauseating. Doug, however, didn't give up on topics that might interest Ronnie.

"Are you a sports enthusiast?" asked Doug. Ronnie became animated. I guess he was.

"How do you think the New England team will do this season in football? asked Doug.

Bingo!!!! Ronnie took his hand off Mother's.

I have season tickets to see the Patriots this season." His face lit up like a neon sign.

Doug was doing pretty well himself. "I had them last year, but we decided they were too expensive." He looked sideways at Joan. She gave him a sympathetic look. I knew not getting season tickets this year had been hard for Doug. As a compromise, they had decided to buy them every other year.

Joan and I sat there, waiting for our Mother to make a move. By now, Timmy was in the living room watching cartoons. And Ronnie and Doug were sitting next to each other, deep in conversation about their favorite team.

"Girls, let's go into the library now. I want to talk with you."

Mother is a person of many moods. It was impossible to read her now as Joan and I followed her into her family room. Mother insisted on calling it the library, but the last time I was in the room, there wasn't a book to be found.

She had changed the furniture around. I sat in a small grouping of chairs by the window. Joan drew up the chair next to me. Mother stood. She again told us how good it was to have the family together. "There's only the five of us, and we must support each other."

My Mother started pacing. She turned to us and started to speak. She stopped.

"Spit it out," I told her.

"OK, here goes. The health club is going to cost a lot more than Ronnie and I thought."

"Do you have the land?" Joan asked.

Mother said they had looked at several parcels. The land was the least of the cost. The equipment they would need and the labor in the construction of the health club would be exorbitant.

"How much?" asked Joan.

Mother looked like she might cry. "Two hundred thousand dollars would put us in good shape."

I felt sorry for Mother. This had been a dream she and Ronnie had, but it hadn't worked out.

"I'm sorry it didn't work out," I said.

"Well, it could."

Both Joan and I chorused our question. "How."

"I can take the money your father left me. Ronnie and I could take a loan on the rest. But we will need operating expenses. That's where you girls come in."

I sat frozen in my chair. What was that all about?

"What do you mean?? You'll take the money Dad left you and put it into one venture as crazy as the health club."

"Allison, calm down. Hear me out."

"I'm trying to stay calm. Dad left that money to you so you could live the rest of your life in comfort without worrying about where your next meal is coming from. Now you're going to blow it on Charles Atlas in the other room."

"I won't have you talking about Ronnie like that. We are deeply in love."

"The only thing he loves is your money," I said, ignoring Joan's, warning looks. "

"If you're going to be like that, I'm not going to talk to you."

One look at Joan told me she would be the quiet, compliant daughter again.t Sometimes, maybe I didn't give Joan a chance because I was so quick to give opinions, but I needed my sister on my side now, and it didn't look like it was going that way. There were times I thought Joan enjoyed my being heavy. Tears came to my eyes.

"Mother, I just got fired. Joan and Doug are working two jobs to make the bills. Have you ever thought of anyone but yourself?"

Mother was furious. "Your father was very generous with you girls. I realize the mutual funds you have are yours, and your father meant for them to pave a brighter future for you. But, don't you see, this is it. By investing in the health club, you'll get your money back with interest."

I laughed. "You've got to be kidding?"

"It's true, Allison. You and Joan will have shares in the club, and as it expands, so will your investment."

"Shit."

"Well, it's true. Allison, you're always so hotheaded. Why don't you listen to what Ronnie and I have to say about the health club? It's going to be the prize of Sandy Ridge.

I shot out of the chair. "What are you thinking?"

Joan stood up. "Calm down, Allison. Let's see what they have to say."

"I don't want to hear what testosterone Charlie has to say." I started for the door.

"This could be a huge success. Well, never mind," said Mother. "Doug and Joan will reap the benefits, and you'll be left hanging as always. With your temper, I'm not surprised you got fired." Leave it to Mother to give a parting shot.

I turned, not wanting Mother to get the parting shot. "Just once," I said, "I'd like to see you do something unselfish. But instead, you always have your hand out. There's no way I'm going to give you Dad's money that he left me. And, if there's any way I can stop you from spending what he left you, I'll do it."

I ran out of the room. Mother ran after me, screaming. "I deserve that money. It's mine. Your Father was a drunken bastard, and I earned that money."

I got to the front door, grabbed my jacket and fled. I had trouble maneuvering the door handle since tears blurred my vision. Ronnie came down to the foyer. His face registered concern.

"Leaving? Can't we talk about this?"

"You creep. You won't be getting any of my money, so forget it."

I pushed past him, fumbled for my car keys, jumped in and hot-footed it out of there.

CHAPTER 15

My mind raced as I drove back to my condo. How could my Mother ask such a thing of Joan and me? Our Father left the money to Joan and me, and I knew he had left plenty to Mother. She was taking too much of a gamble, putting all of hers into a health club. Mother didn't have any business sense, and Ronnie didn't look like he did. This would bomb, and they would be left with no money. Then Mother would come and live with me. Ugh. What a thought. I wanted never to bother with Mother again, and certainly wasn't going to give her my money.

I pulled over to the side of the road and did some deep breathing. My body was trembling. I closed my eyes and tried to relax. Soon, my pulse became regular. I should try this more often. My thoughts strayed to better days. The time when my Father was alive, he was off the booze, and Mother was taking care of him.

My eyes were getting heavy. Dusk was settling over the car like storm clouds just before rain. I started my car and continued home.

It was eight thirty when I got home. My living room was a mess with old newspapers on the floor. I collected them and took them to the recyclable bin.

Coming back into my front door, looking at the dust on the furniture, I got a cloth and polish. One swish and the table was clean. Then I tackled the other one and then the coffee table. How did everything get so dusty? It made me feel lousy that I wasn't domestic enough to keep my home cleaner, so I tried to rationalize that some people were better at housework than others. If Mother saw this, she would really let into me. Thinking of Mother and what happened this evening, I scrubbed harder. The glass was Mother, and I was trying to eradicate her. Only, I didn't really, if you know what I mean.

The phone rang. I knew it was probably Joan, and I didn't want to talk to her, so I let the answering machine get it. Joan's passivity with Mother fried me. When Joan and I were together, she was sarcastic about things Mother did, but as soon as our Mother was around, Joan was agreeable as all get out. My mind strayed back to tonight, and Joan saying, "Oh, Mother, this pie is delicious." Ugh.

I was right. "Pick up, Allison   . I know you're there. Please pick up."

I tackled my end tables with a vengeance. Then I started in on the windows. Might as well get everything while I was in the mood.

I was finishing up when my intercom buzzer rang. It was Ted. Had I forgotten a date we had? No. Ted took a chance I might be home. Damn him for taking me for granted.

I ran to the bathroom mirror to see how I looked. I combed my hair and put lipstick on.

What kept you so long?" he asked, irritated.

CHAPTER 16

I kissed him lightly and smiled up at him. "How come you're so grumpy?"

"It's been a busy day."

"You want a drink?" I asked, moving to the hutch. "Scotch and water," he answered and sat down.

I got him his drink and a soft drink for myself, sitting next to him on the couch. By now, he was surfing the TV. He found wrestling. Oh, joy!

I asked Ted about his day, but he grumbled something about not wanting to talk about it. After several other attempts to make conversation, it became apparent he was not interested in talking.

"Did you come over to see me or to watch the wrestling matches?" He didn't hear me, or if he did, he ignored me.

I sat there for a while, trying to get interested in what was going on. I moved closer to Ted, looking for a cuddle. He turned to me and asked if I had any chips to munch on.

"Go to hell!" I shouted. "I'm going to bed. Make sure the door is locked when you leave."

I went into the bedroom, got undressed and got ready for bed. When the wrestling was over, he'd leave. He did that sometimes when I had an early morning, and he had a day off or was going in later.

After reading, I went into the bathroom to brush my teeth. He was cheering those damn wrestlers on. He didn't even know I wasn't there. Snuggling under the covers, I realized what my heart had known for a long time. Ted wouldn't change, and I must move on. Muffy joined me, and I soon fell asleep.

I was awakened by a wet kiss on my cheek. It was Ted. "What the.... "I said groggily.

I looked at the clock on the bedside table.

"Ted, what do you think you're doing at one o'clock in the morning?"

He kissed me harder, his tongue reaching into my mouth. His body was on mine, which I might have enjoyed had he not reeked of alcohol. I jumped up.

"Let's continue what we started the other night," he slurred.

"Get out, Ted, and don't bother coming back," I yelled.

Ted stared at me glassy-eyed, trying to figure out if I meant business. "What the hell is it with you dames? First you want it, then you don't. Who the hell can figure you out."

I'd never seen Ted this ugly. And he was stinking drunk. I didn't say anything. I couldn't. Then, as quickly as he got mad, he shrugged his shoulders and got off the bed. "OK, babe, but you'll be sorry in the morning."

I motioned for him to get out. I followed him into the hall and made sure he left, locking the door behind him and got into bed. I felt used and disgusted. When would I ever find a guy that cared about me? The tears came in sobs until, finally, I slept.

The next thing I knew, the sun was piercing through my vertical drapes. It was ten o'clock. I was sluggish, got my coffee and returned to bed, turning my TV on to the local cable channel talk show. I sat up in surprise as I saw Sandy Ridge's Police Chief Ed Hall. He was being grilled about the murder of a girl called Blaire Nugent. The interviewer was a cute blond with a perky disposition usually, but she was sober today, asking Hall about developments in the case that had reached national headlines.

Hall showed a composite drawing of what the girl could have looked like at one time. "There were many knife marks on her face. Whoever killed her didn't want us to trace her identity because there were knife marks to the pads of her fingers also," explained Hall, "so we had trouble tracing her fingerprints."

The news commentator looked appropriately sympathetic.

"This murder happened several months back. Has the trail gotten cold? Should our viewers be concerned there is a psychotic killer loose in tranquil Sandy Ridge?? I thought the only thing people worried about in that sleepy town was the time of high tide?"

Hall squirmed in his seat a bit. "This is not a random killing. Whoever murdered Blaire Nugent wanted her dead. They were looking for her and, unfortunately, found her. As for Sandy Ridge, it's full of caring and kind people who hate this as much as anyone.

Come over sometime, and I'll give you a tour. We are all very proud of our town."

The commentator nodded her head. "Is this a crime that will go unsolved for lack of evidence?" asked the woman, baiting Hall.

Hall reassured her that the killer or killers of Blaire Nugent would be found and the police would not stop investigating until they had."

"My sources close to the case have said that you now have two Blaire Nugents in Sandy Ridge," the newswoman said. "One has been murdered, and one has disappeared. That is a bizarre turn of the case, isn't it?"

Hall admitted there were two women named Blaire Nugent. The real Blaire was the murdered girl, and the other girl was a "Person of interest," and they wanted to talk to her, but she had mysteriously disappeared. Police were following leads to track her down, hoping she might have information that would help them in the case.

"We know that the murdered girl is Blaire Nugent, Chief," said the interviewer. "Why would someone take her name, and is this imposter a suspect in the case?"

Hall said he wasn't at liberty to disclose the case.

"What now?" the woman asked.

"We do have clues to run down, and we're asking the public's help. That's why I'm here today. The murdered woman worked as a newspaper reporter in Quincy, Massachusetts, a city south of Boston. She may have had ties to that community, and we're asking anyone to come forward that may have known her." Hall turned in his chair and looked straight into the TV cameras. He looked pretty sharp, and the interviewer had not got the best of him as she sometimes did with guests on the show.

"Somebody has to be missing this woman who left Quincy and came to Sandy Ridge," said Hall. "We hope to reach that person who may be watching now, and hopefully, they will come forward.

The TV host thanked Hall for appearing on her show and shook his hand politely. I turned the TV off after Hall's segment of the show.

The murdered woman worked as a newspaper reporter in Quincy, Massachusetts.

My former roommate not only took her name her occupation, but also where she lived before coming to Sandy Ridge. It sounds more and more like she killed the real Blaire Nugent. But why take every bit of her identity, even down to the place she worked?

I sat on the bed, sipping my coffee, staring obliquely at the TV screen.

"Muffy, where did I put my maps?" I had a GPS but felt more secure having maps with me.

My cat looked at me with a stare that said she couldn't keep track of everything for me.

Muffy followed me out to the kitchen, however, in case I wanted to put some turkey from the deli in her bowl. I had other things on my mind, though, as I rummaged through my junk drawers for the maps, which I found.

My cat walked away.

Spreading the map out on the kitchen table, I found Quincy and circled it with a pen, highlighting the best route to drive. Satisfied I could get to Quincy, I went into my bedroom, grabbed my suitcase off the top shelf of my closet and packed in case I had to stay over. I was going to Quincy. I didn't know what I would find, but I knew I had to try to find out what happened to my roommate.

CHAPTER 17

Once packed, I grabbed another cup of coffee to take on the road. I called my neighbor Margie to feed Muffy. Once I had lost my keys, she helped me, and I made an extra key, so if that happened again, all I had to do was get them from her. The traffic was getting heavier coming through Boston due to commuters, but there were plenty of signs directing me to Quincy, so I had no trouble finding it, although I did take a wrong turn and found myself in a residential neighborhood. The houses were clean and had a fresh look to them. The grass was mowed. It looked like a typical neighborhood in Sandy Ridge. I saw signs for a hospital and followed those, figuring that it would be close to the center of town. I was right and found myself on Hancock Street, a busy main drag. Blaire Nugent had worked for the Quincy Sentinel. I took out my GPS, followed directions, and a friendly voice was soon telling me what to do. I saw my days of getting lost were clearly behind me.

The Quincy Sentinel was a ten-story brick building with a lot of windows. Shrubs and colorful plants dotted the entrance. I looked at my watch. It was three o'clock, and my stomach told me I needed to eat. Fortunately for me, Burger King was across the street. I went in and ordered myself a diet Coke, French fries and a grilled chicken sandwich. It was delicious. As I ate, I wondered how I would present myself at The Quincy Sentinel. Should I inquire if Blaire Nugent works there as if I didn't know she was dead?

Neither appeared to be satisfactory since her murder had made National news.

I finished my lunch wanting more. It would have to wait. I left my car where it was parked and crossed the street. Out of nowhere, a car came gunning down the street. I hurried across. I reached the curb, but the car kept coming. Was it out of control?

It's funny how instincts take over at a time like that. I jumped into one of the hedges, which surprised me because I flunked gym in school. Athletic. I'm not. I actually felt the breeze of the car going past me. The car stopped, backed up and skidded away.

Crazy driver. It happened so fast I didn't have time to make out the license plate or the model of the car.

I was in the middle of this shrub, the prickly ends of which were sticking into private parts of my body, and I attempted to catch my breath. My heart beat rapidly, and dizziness overcame me. In the limited space, sitting in the bush, I put my head between my knees and breathed deeply. I willed myself not to faint.

I stayed in the bush for what seemed like a long time, but it was only ten minutes. Looking around to see if the car was coming back, I saw the skid marks in the road. I realized what a narrow escape I had had. I'm OK, I told myself. Let's concentrate on Blaire right now and chalk it up to a crazy driver. I looked around to see if there were witnesses to what had just happened. No such luck. I removed myself from the bush as delicately as possible and took inventory of my clothes. They didn't appear to be torn, although I did have scratches on my arms and legs. I adjusted myself and assessed my surroundings.

The Quincy Sentinel was the first of many buildings on the street that looked like professional buildings. Big bucks had gone into the landscaping and building of the newspaper.

Inside, a pretty girl who looked like she should still be in high school was manning the information desk in the middle of the lobby. She reminded me of "Barbie," and I wanted to ask her where "Ken" was, but I restrained myself. She even smiled like a "Barbie" when I approached her.

"May I help you?"

I said I was looking for the suburban editor. That seemed like a good place to start.

"Barbie" told me he was on the third floor, and she directed me to the elevators. I thanked her profusely. I also asked for the editor's name. She looked blank and confessed she didn't know. I assured her it was OK.

Newspaper offices look all alike. Somewhere along the line, someone must have decided this would be the way they looked, and nobody has had the guts to change them since.

The Quincy Sentinel had their staff reporters in cubbies, just like The Courier.

People were rushing around with pieces of paper in their hands. Reporters were glued to their computer screens. Telephones were ringing incessantly.

A sadness and loneliness filled my heart. I missed being at The Courier. I brushed it aside. Right now, I have more important business to do.

I stood on the other side of a circular desk and waited for someone to notice me. It took a few minutes, and then a slim older woman approached me.

"May I help you?" she asked, half smiling.

I did her better and returned a whole smile. "Yes. I'd like to talk to your suburban editor."

She looked around. "He was here a minute ago." The woman spied him and yelled, "Jack." He turned around, and she motioned him over.

When he came to us, the woman turned and said, "I don't believe I know your name."

"Allison Peters. I'm a staff reporter with The Courier in Sandy Ridge, Maine." I knew I needed some leverage. A little lie didn't hurt.

She introduced me to Jack Dawson, and while he and I shook hands, she quietly withdrew.

Do all editors have to be middle-aged and paunchy? That was Jack Dawson. He was better looking than Shaw, but he needed to lose 50 pounds or so. I think editors put on weight because they aren't out there anymore chasing the story. Anyway, Jack Dawson had a nice smile. Shaw still needed to work on his.

Dawson shook my hand and asked me to come into his office. "Are you here to interview for the staff reporter's job?" he asked.

"No," I said, "I'm here to ask you about Blaire Nugent."

He stared at me. It took him a minute to get the connection between Sandy Ridge, Maine, and my being there. "I've already told the police everything I know about Blaire. Please leave, or I'll have to call security."

I was taken aback by his attitude and told him so.

"Look, Blaire was a good reporter. She did her job. I didn't know anything about her personal life,"

"Did she hang out with any girls from the newsroom?" I asked. "Did she have a boyfriend?"

Dawson got up. "My reporters don't socialize at work. They work hard, and those that don't aren't here long."

What a sweetheart!

The editor opened the door for me. The interview was over. I stood. "What story was she working on, or was she in Maine for a story?"

"I don't know. Sorry, I couldn't help."

I bet you are.

Once outside his office, something told me not to leave quite yet. The water fountain was around the corner from Dawson's office, outside the restroom. I went over and took a drink.

I heard Dawson call someone, and they started talking. Ever so cautiously, I peered around the corner. Dawson was talking to a tall, young, good-looking guy in his thirties and had his back to me. The men doubled back to the guy's desk, deep in conversation.

I went into the Ladies' Room. Luck was with me. There was a young woman around my age washing her hands. She looked at me in the mirror and smiled.

"Hi," I said. "I'm a relative of Blaire Nugent's, and I came into the newspaper to meet her friends and thank them for coming to her funeral," I rattled on, not daring to stop lest the woman think I was phony.

The girl accepted my story and started talking. "Isn't it awful about poor Blaire? I'm so sorry for your loss. She was a great gal."

"Did you know her well?" I asked hopefully.

"We went out for pizza, sometimes, on payday."

"Who else went?'

"All of us girls and sometimes the guys." I was really getting into this. "I'm glad Blaire had friends to hang out with."

"Well, Mary Engels was her best friend. They went everywhere together. You must have met her at the wake. I couldn't go because I worked the late shift, but I was at the funeral."

"There were so many people there and, of course, I was so sad, I don't remember. The faces just ran in together," I said.

She studied me. "It's funny, I was introduced to all the family. I don't remember you."

Don't panic, I told myself.

"Tell me, is Mary Engels working today?" I asked.

"Yeah. Do you remember her from the funeral?"

"Oh, sure."

The girl offered to show me where Mary worked. As an afterthought, she introduced herself as Beth Daniels and again told me how sorry she was for my loss.

I put on my sad face and told her I was happy to meet any friend of Blaire's, and we left the Ladies' Room. Following Beth into the newsroom, I looked around for Dawson. He wasn't in his office. I knew I had a short time before Dawson caught up with me, since he wouldn't have let me talk to Mary Engels.

So, intent was my search. I almost ran into Beth as she stopped at a desk.

Beth introduced me to Mary Engels. She turned to look at me. "What was your relationship to Blaire anyway? You never did tell me."

My mind went blank. Four eyes were staring at me now. "Uh, cousins, we were cousins," I said, my voice catching.

Mary Engels smiled. She looked like a happy person who smiled often. Mary extended her hand. I took it and introduced myself, deciding to use my own name. I needed this woman's help and needed to be honest with her. A little bit, anyway.

I liked Mary Engels at once. She was taller than Beth, smaller in structure, but a little heavier. I gauged her to be in her middle thirties. Mary had short, curly brown hair and big brown eyes, more pronounced by mascara and curly eyelashes.

I thanked my lucky stars when Beth left, should I get caught in any more lies, since, at this point, I didn't remember what I had told her. I was so nervous.

Mary asked me to sit down. I kept wondering where Dawson was, trying casually to look around every now and then, realizing I didn't have that much time before being found out.

"How well did you know Blaire?" I began.

Tears sprang to Mary's eyes. "I loved her. She was a sweet, talented person."

"How so?"

"Good nose for news, as we say in the business. But she was compassionate and thorough, always checked her sources, and always got the other side of the story. Blaire was a special person who liked everyone."

"Someone didn't like her, that's for sure."

"A terrible tragedy, to be so young with her life ahead of her," said Mary, shaking her head.

"Did she have a boyfriend?"

"Darren Quill. She was crazy about him and vice versa, from what I understood.

"It was so sad to see him at the funeral. He couldn't stop crying."

"I wasn't very close to Blaire. Something about our mothers not getting along, so I hardly ever saw Blaire, but when I did, we got along very well."

The noise was deafening. Both Mary and I jumped.

"Miss Peters, what the hell do you think you're doing?" Dawson yelled in my ear.

Mary looked scared. I couldn't blame her, and I felt bad for the reporters who had to work with this editor. Shaw was brusque, but he didn't yell, so the heavens fell down. Dawson sounded like a bastard. Mary's hands were shaking. Her face was white with fear, and I was pissed that anyone should have such an effect on their employees. For all Dawson knew, Mary could have been a long-lost friend of mine that I hadn't seen for years and had discovered accidentally while I was here.

I stayed in my seat deliberately. Actually, I was trying to get my wits about me. Mary stared at me questioningly. Dawson moved to my side. If he touched me, he was dead meat.

Counting to ten slowly, I rose from my chair. Without a word, Dawson pointed to the door. His face was red. When I passed him, I detected a perspiration smell and noticed a wetness under his arm pointed at me. No need to mention that. I turned and left, walking slowly with my head high. I could feel his seething breath as I passed him.

Chapter 18

Outside in my car, I couldn't figure out why Dawson had been so upset. Poor Mary looked scared. He wouldn't fire her, would he? I decided to stay over and see Darren Quill. A Marriott wasn't too far away, and I checked in for one night. My room on the fourth floor was a typical hotel room: two queen-sized beds, a TV, two bureaus, a desk with a telephone and an additional one in the bathroom next to the toilet. The room service menu looked yummy, but first, I needed to connect with Darren Quill. There were two in the phone book, which I thought was strange, considering it wasn't a common name. I held my breath that his number wasn't unlisted. I hit pay dirt on the first attempt.

"Darren Quill, please."

"Speaking."

"Darren, I'm a friend of Blaire Nugent. First, I want to extend my sympathy to you for the murder of your girlfriend. The police will find the person who did it. I was hoping we might meet to talk about Blaire."

He was quiet. "What's your name?"

I told him.

He said nothing.

"Are you there?"

"How do I know you're not one of those nosy newspaper reporters wanting to get yet another story about Blaire?"

I didn't dare tell him I was a reporter. Even a fired one. The way he was acting, he wouldn't believe it.

"Please," I pleaded. "Blaire was my roommate in Sandy Ridge, Maine, for a short time before she was killed. She seemed to be a nice person. Certainly, nobody deserves what happened to her. If we meet, maybe the two of us can better understand what went down and why.

"I'm at the Marriott on South Street. I'm not sure where you live. This is my first trip to Quincy. Are you able to meet me here at my hotel in the bar downstairs in an hour?"

He reluctantly agreed. "If you're not on the up and up, I will give you trouble like you've never seen,"

I couldn't blame him. He was in mourning for his girlfriend. He probably had the police and newspapers on his back, but I needed to find out what happened to the real Blaire Nugent, and it felt like I had hit pay dirt with Darren Quill.

Blaire's friend Mary said the couple dated. Were they close enough that Darren could give me insight into Blaire.......and maybe Shaw? Where the hell had that come from? I cautioned myself not to get too excited. The whole evening could fizzle.

One check in the bedroom mirror, a comb-through and lipstick, and I was ready. Hungry, I went down to the bar early. That way, I could see Darren Quill before he saw me and size him up. He had said he was six feet three inches tall, had dark hair and wore glasses. He would be in a gray hoodie, blue shirt and blue denims. I had told him what I looked like. Unless there was a baseball game tonight and a lot of guys were hanging out for the evening, there wouldn't be much trouble spotting him.

Downstairs, the bar had dark paneling round tables with four or five chairs around each table. A pretty good piano player was in a comer playing oldies but goodies. I love appetizers such as chicken wings, and they were free tonight until eight o'clock. I rationalized eating so many of the appetizers since I was on a limited budget, but I ordered a Caesar salad with anchovies. The waitress gave me a strange look when I asked for more appetizers, but Darren Quill might not have eaten. I called him around six thirty. He said he'd meet me around eight. It was seven-thirty now. The next hour I spent watching people. By ten thirty, I had lost my taste for Diet Coke, and my stomach said I was full. But no, Darren Quill. I guess he wasn't coming. It probably was too painful to talk to anyone, especially a stranger.

At eleven, I started to leave when I felt someone's presence around me. "Darren?" A guy came off a corner stool. He was tall, wore sunglasses and had dark hair.

"How long have you been checking me out?" I asked. "If you knew who I was, why didn't you come over?"

I wasn't sure."

"Was it because you knew who I was, but you didn't know whether to talk to me or not?"

He shrugged. "A bit of both, I suppose."

I was weary but couldn't let him get away. "Give me ten minutes, let me explain my situation, then you can walk if you want."

Darren stared at me. "Please."

"Let's get a quiet table over there," Quill said, leading the way.

A waitress came over and introduced herself. Quill looked at me. I ordered another diet soft drink, and he, a beer.

The waitress set our drinks before us. Quill waited until she left. "Well?" he demanded.

I told him about the girl who became my roommate, who called herself Blaire Nugent, and how, shortly after living with me, she disappeared.

"What did she look like?"

I described her and how, after that, police found a body that turned out to be the real Blaire Nugent. Quill winced. I told him how my condo was broken into and my roommate's things taken.

The waitress came over to see how everything was. Quill ordered another beer. I passed and wondered how many beers he had already had.

Too many. His eyes were red, and he was getting surly. Had he gotten surly with Blaire and accidentally killed her?

Quill took a big gulp of his beer. He leaned closer to me. The smell of beer had never been a turn-on. It wasn't now.

"It sounds like Blaire's sister was your former roommate," he said.

"But why would she do that?"

He shrugged. "Who knows why Susan would do anything."

"Is that her name?"

Quill nodded. "Susan was always getting into trouble, " Blaire said. She felt badly for her and tried to straighten her out. But Susan wouldn't listen. Susan had gotten into drugs.. She had a real drinking problem. She traveled with the wrong crowd. Blaire wanted her to go to rehab."

The guy in front of me started picking at the skin around his nails. It was then I noticed his nails were down to the quick with some dried blood around them. He must chew his nails, I thought. He drinks to excess, chews his nails, he slumps over. This guy was a mess.

"What kind of drugs? Was she into crime?"

"I never knew. But I think Blaire did because Blaire was upset the last time I saw her. When I asked her what was wrong, she wouldn't tell me. She knew I didn't like Susan, and I resented her taking so much of Blaire's time."

"Where did Susan live?"

"In Quincy, not far from Blaire. That was part of the problem. I was trying to get Blaire to move in with me and get married, but Blaire had some crazy idea she should be helping her sister."

"Because they were sisters?"

Darren snickered.

I looked at him questionably to explain.

"There couldn't have been more different sisters. Susan was conniving, manipulative......."

"They hadn't known each other long," I said.

Blaire's boyfriend looked at me and then at his watch. He rose to leave. "Please," I begged. "Tell me all of what you know. There is a connection. I know it."

He sat down. "I just can't believe Susan would kill Blaire, even with all her faults. They were thrilled to find each other."

I was excited by this news and asked Darren to explain.

"Blaire found Susan after much searching. She hired a private detective that specializes in finding lost siblings once she discovered she had a sister."

"When was that?"

"Three years ago. I'll start at the beginning." Quill hailed the waitress and looked at me. I shook my head. His hands were trembling. His right knee was going at a fast clip, too.

I wanted to somehow comfort this guy, but I knew he was skittish. So, I just waited for him to continue.

Our waitress came back. He took a sip of his new brew.

"Blaire and Susan were born a couple of years apart. They were put in different foster homes. They never knew about each other. Their mother was an unwed mother who evidently didn't learn the first time. Two years later, she gets knocked up again."

I nodded.

"Anyway, it was the same guy. Can you believe that? He didn't want to marry her the first time. I guess she didn't even ask the second.

"The mother went to a home for unwed mothers. When the mother gave birth, she put the babies in foster care and later gave them up. How stupid can you be?"

"Why do you say that?" I asked.

"Imagine the woman, Susan and Blaire's mother, being so stupid as to get pregnant again? Why didn't she dump the guy when he didn't want to marry her after the first baby?" Darren's face was contorted in anger. He pounded the table. The waitress came over.

"Is something wrong, Sir?" she asked.

Blaire's boyfriend looked at her like he might belt her, so I rushed in. "My friend was only making a point, and he got a little bit excited. I'll have another Diet Coke. How about you, Darren?"

He ordered another. "Where was I?"

"You were talking about Blaire's biological mother. But let's move on. It sounds like you have strong feelings against the mother."

"To hear Susan talk, she hated her foster parents, who apparently were physically and verbally abusive. At least that's what she told Blaire. An uncle molested her at nine years old.

"Blaire, on the other hand, has.... uh, had good memories of her foster care. Only Blaire was adopted?"

I asked Quill if his girlfriend had always been interested in knowing who her real mother was.

Darren told me Blaire had gone up into her foster parent's attic one day. She did that often, found the seclusion peaceful and often wrote poetry and short stories up there. "One day, Blaire was looking through some old papers and found her birth certificate.

With it was a letter from the children's service organization. The letter mentioned a sister. Blaire didn't want to discuss this information with her adoptive parents."

"Why not?"

"She didn't want to hurt their feelings about what she was about to do because she contacted a detective agency who, actually, found Susan in a relatively short time, six months.

"But I thought that information was confidential.?"

Quill shrugged. He did that a lot. "I think if the biological mother writes a letter stating that if the kids come looking for her, she is giving permission to do that."

"And Blaire's mother gave permission?" I asked.

"Apparently not to find the mother. Blaire still didn't know who that was, but the mother gave permission for the sisters to find each other."

I thought that was strange, but I didn't want to interrupt Quill in his story. "So, Blaire looked Susan up?"

Darren nodded.

"And what happened?" This was going very slow.

"They met. It went well, but Blaire said that Susan was really hard up. She didn't have money for her rent, so Blaire asked Susan to move in with her. I told Blaire not to move so fast in their relationship. Maybe check up on Susan, ya know, first. But Blaire was so excited about finding her sibling ya couldn't talk to her. So, Susan moved in.

That's when I got to know Susan better. She had a mouth on her like you wouldn't believe. Blaire kept telling me to be patient, but the difference between Blaire and Susan was huge, and I didn't want Blaire to get hurt."

"Was your girlfriend always that trusting?"

I tried to put myself in Blaire's shoes and had to admit her reaction would have been mine.

Darren shrugged. "Well, about two months after Susan and Blaire had an awful fight about a job Susan was going to take. Susan had met a woman at a bar who proposed something shady. Susan, I guess, was out of money. Blaire didn't want Susan to do anything illegal.

"Despite what Blaire told her, Susan moved out. Blaire was frantic. She had found her sister and wasn't going to lose her. The last time I saw Blaire, we fought. I told her to stop trying to find Susan and marry me. I ended up stomping out, and Blaire went to find her sister.

Darren said he knew something was wrong the next day when any attempts to call his girlfriend were futile. He had a key to her place and went over. "Blaire's things were gone," said Darren, his eyes filling up with tears.

"I wish I could bring Blaire back to you."

He acted as if he hadn't heard. "Blaire wouldn't tell me where Susan was going, although I think she knew. When I saw the headlines in the newspaper about my girl's death," Quill choked up. I reached out to comfort him. He waved the waitress over for another drink.

"Getting drunk won't help."

"When I drink, I don't feel the pain as much."

"I'm sorry," was all I could say. "Do you want a ride somewhere?"

He shrugged that suggestion off. "I'm OK." He stood up and walked, or staggered, back to the bar.

I got up and left the bar, turning once to look back at Quill. He was staring into his drink as if it had all the answers. I continued on out to the front desk and told them I would be staying another week.

Then I went back to the bar. After an hour of convincing Quill, he consented to go home in a cab. I put him in the taxi myself, paid the driver, went upstairs, and fell asleep on the bed in my clothes.

CHAPTER 19

I quickly found out Quincy was not Sandy Ridge. In fact, it appeared gigantic. I found myself getting more frustrated by the minute because of the one-way streets and the crazy drivers who thought they were on a speedway.

Blaire's parents lived on the Braintree side of Quincy. I noticed I was empty and filled up at the nearest station. It was two o'clock. I needed to stop and get something to eat but decided on a drive-thru since I didn't want my stomach to growl while I was talking to the Nugent's. 1 reached my destination in twenty minutes and popped a piece of gum into my mouth in case I had bad breath.

The house was a modest Cape, with vinyl siding and black trim. Dormers, probably bedrooms, looked out onto the street. A nice house, I thought, as I rang the bell.

The bell chimed on and on. I detected a melody that was familiar, but I couldn't place it. That would be maddening after a while, I thought. A doorbell should be concise and tell those inside that someone is visiting them, not be a prelude to a concert. I waited. No one came.

I don't give up that easily. I knocked loudly on the door, which was immediately opened by a tall, slim woman with black hair. She had jeans and a black sweatshirt with yellow flowers on the front. She wore what looked like comfortable walking shoes. I noticed all of this because I tried to keep my eyes off her face, which was red. The woman's eyes were swollen, and my heart went out to her.

"May I help you?" she asked. Tissues clutched her right hand.

"My name is Allison Peters. I'm from Sandy Ridge, Maine."

The woman's look was resigned. She sighed. Another person to intrude on her privacy. I knew I needed to talk fast.

"I would like to talk to you about Blaire," I said.

"Are you from the press?" she asked. "They have been hounding me, and I would appreciate you leaving my family alone."

"I have worked for a newspaper, but I'm not here for a story. I'm here because I need to understand what happened to your daughter." I hoped I sounded convincing.

The woman started to close the door. "Please," I begged.

"What was my daughter to you?" she asked.

"That's what I'm trying to find out," I said. She looked perplexed, but not as much as I was. "Listen, can we start again?" I asked. "I knew a girl who called herself Blaire Nugent, but when your daughter was found, I knew that person had been lying to me. That girl has disappeared, and I know it has something to do with your daughter.

"Please help me shed some light on this confusing situation."

Blaire's mother hesitated, then stood aside. "Come in," she said, sighing again. I rushed in, lest she change her mind.

The carpet in the foyer felt new and plush under my feet. Mrs. Nugent directed me to the living room. It was a lived-in room, comfortable yet elegant somehow with its colorful vases and glass coffee table and end tables. A book was on its spine, and several magazines were on the coffee table. A coaster was under a half-filled glass with a can of soda next to it.

I passed pictures of what I knew must be Blaire. Someone liked oriental since the couch and the armchairs were splashy, vibrant colors that enhanced the beauty of the carpet that extended into the living room.

"Please sit down," Blaire's mother offered. "Would you like anything to drink, tea, coffee?"

I declined.

We stared at each other for a couple of seconds. I hadn't really rehearsed what I would say if I met Blaire's parents.

"I'm sorry about your daughter," I began.

Mrs. Nugent nodded, her eyes spilling over with tears. "Were you friends with my daughter?" she asked gently.

"No," I answered. "I never knew your daughter, Mrs. Nugent, like I told you, but somehow I have a connection to her, which I'm trying to understand."

She looked at me quizzically. I hurried on, reiterating what I had said. "I met a girl in Sandy Ridge that I took in as a roommate. She called herself Blaire Nugent, yet she wasn't your daughter.

I reached over and took her hand. "I'm so sorry I had to come here today and dredge up the terrible circumstances of your daughter's death."

She took a minute to compose herself. "Just what is it you want to know?"

"Why did your daughter go to Sandy Ridge?"

She rose from her chair and started pacing. "That's what her father and I are trying to figure out. She'd never been to Sandy Ridge. I don't know what possessed her to go there," the woman said, shaking her head. She continued pacing as if the motion kept her grief at bay.

"Did she know anybody in Maine that she could have been visiting?" I asked, hating myself for hammering at her.

She didn't look at me. She looked to my left as if expecting the answers there. She covered her face, then took her hands away and looked at me. Her face was contorted in anger. Tears were streaming down her face. "I know that bitch had something to do with it."

"Who are you talking about?" I asked.

The woman sat down, started to cry, and shook her fist. "Nothing was the same once that bitch came here."

"Tell me about it, Mrs. Nugent." I kept my voice low and unemotional. The rage on the woman's face was real. She was sobbing now, and I somehow felt responsible.

Blaire's mother was gasping for breath.

I left the room and found the kitchen. I got her a glass of water. "Here, take this," I said.

She did as I told her, water spilling out the sides of her mouth.

"Slowly," I said. I knelt down in front of her. She looked at me, her eyes spilling out with tears. "My baby's dead. My baby's dead." Blaire's mother started screaming and pulling her hair. I grabbed hold of her and hugged her. I wept as I held her tight. I wept for her pain, for a nice woman who raised a nice daughter.

Chapter 20

I consoled Blaire's mother until her sobs became hiccups. I led her over to the couch and had her lie down. When I stood up, she pleaded for me to stay with her. I assured her I would and asked if she wanted me to call anyone to be with her. According to the hall clock, an hour had passed since I rang the Nugent's doorbell. The woman on the couch was exhausted and closed her eyes. I reached over the back of the couch and covered her with a coverlet.

Suddenly, the front door opened, and a tall guy entered, newspaper in hand. He took a defensive stand when he saw me after looking at the figure on the couch who was now sleeping. I quickly moved to his side and introduced myself extending my hand. Mr. Nugent ignored it.

I quickly told him I was a friend of his daughter's and had come to pay my respects.

He looked around for his wife and went over to the couch. "What have you done to my wife?"

"Your wife and I were talking about Blaire. She looked like she had been crying before I came, so when we started talking about Blaire, your wife started crying again.

"I feel badly I upset her," I apologized. "She cried herself out, and when she was calmer, I suggested she lay on the couch. As you can see, she's sleeping."

I assured him she was OK. He woke her up anyway. I couldn't blame him. She looked terrible. Her face was red blotches. Her clothes were disheveled.

Mrs. Nugent stirred and stared up at both of us. She had no idea where she was. "Sit up, honey and get your bearings," her husband suggested.

She did. The woman looked at me blankly. Slowly, recognition came across her face.

The woman got up, found some Kleenex, blew her nose, adjusted her clothes and sat down.

Mr. Nugent kissed her tenderly on the forehead, then on the lips. He sat down on the couch and held her hand. He looked at me, his face angry.

I started to speak, but he interrupted. "My wife and I have been through so much in the last six months ; I really don't want her upset any more than she has been. So, please leave." I wanted to stay but didn't dare push it.

He stood up. "Please respect our privacy and not come back. On the way to the front door, I heard Mr. Nugent say to his wife. "I don't know what is to become of us now. Blaire was our whole world."

I turned. "Mr. Nugent, before your wife became so emotional, she talked about someone who came to visit Blaire. I got the idea that she was not welcome, at least not by her."

The man disintegrated before me. "That bitch."

I moved closer. "That's what your wife called her, but I need to know who she was. It may have something to do with who murdered your daughter."

"Blaire was thrilled to meet her," he said. "She's so trusting......" The man caught himself. I nodded, wanting him to know I understood something of what he and his wife were going through.

"Who is Mr. Nugent?"

He looked at me as if seeing me for the first time. "She said her name was Susan." He shrugged. "I don't know. I guess it could have been."

"What?" I asked. "Who is Susan?"

"I asked you to leave. Please, before I have to call the police."

Blaire's father got up. He loomed over me at what must have been over six feet four inches.

I left, not looking back. I did hear him lock the door behind me.

Deflated, I drove back to my hotel, got fast food on the way, watched some TV and went to bed early. The emotion of the afternoon had left me exhausted.

The next day, my stomach felt like a rock. The clock next to my bed said seven o'clock. I turned over and slept until eleven. As I dressed, I toyed with going home to Sandy Ridge. Remembering that woman's devastation yesterday brought me to tears. Who am I to encroach on her grief? Or Blaire's father?

What would I do anyway if I found Blaire's killer? Eggs Benedict and two cups of coffee soothed my nerves, after which I took a walk around the perimeter of the hotel. The sun was out, and it would be a delightful early Spring day. Hyacinths were sprouting. I leaned over to catch the fragrance which I adored. Crocus were patchy now, and the tulips would be open by the end of the day. It gave me optimism to stay on track. I would take it one day at a time, and if l saw I wasn't getting anywhere, I'd leave.

I knew the answers lie with Blaire's mother, and as much as I hated to, I'd have to go back to see her the next day. Blaire's parents had seen Susan. Maybe they could give some clue into why both girls had gone to Maine. My watch said three thirty. I didn't want to run into the father again. It took me only a moment to decide tomorrow would be better.

The next day, I found myself in front of the parent's door with Styrofoam plates in a picnic basket and a thermos of coffee in my hand. It was eleven thirty. I had gotten sandwiches and beverages from the hotel, and they put them in a cute picnic basket. My wish was to ingratiate myself into the mother's good graces.

Her face fell when she saw me, but she opened the door. "Please leave me alone," she said.

"I'm sorry about a couple of days ago. I never meant to upset you. I brought you food as a peace offering. Have you had lunch?"

"No," the woman faltered.

"You must keep your strength up," I began, reaching for the door. The woman held onto the door from inside. But only for a moment, then let me in. "I hope you like ham and cheese," I said. "And coffee?" I held up the thermos.

Once in the house, Blaire's mother indicated we should move into the dining room. I laid out the Styrofoam plates with pickles and potato chips. The woman smiled. "This is nice. I haven't taken the time to eat the last couple of days."

I told her how sorry I was to have upset her the day I was there. "That wasn't my intent. Let's sit down and eat, and I'll tell you why I came to Quincy and how I think you can help me find your daughter's killer.

We both ate with gusto, and I talked about everyday things: the weather and the flowers I had seen earlier. Mrs. Nugent talked about her garden, flowers until snow came and a vegetable garden in summer. She asked me to call her Gwen and remembered my name from the other day.

I began very slowly to explain the reason I had come to Quincy from Sandy Ridge, how I believed now that my roommate was Blaire's sister Susan, and how I thought Blaire's connection with Susan could lead to finding out who killed their daughter. "The last time I was here, both you and your husband called Susan a bitch. So that indicated to me that you met Susan. Could you tell me about her?" I asked.

"She came to the door a year ago, saying she was Blaire's biological sister. We knew Blaire had a sister but never thought the sisters would connect. She fed

Blaire a story about being abused physically and verbally by her foster parents. Our daughter felt sorry for Susan and thought she owed her something because she had such a good life. She wanted Susan to move in. When we refused, pleading with Blaire to investigate Susan's story, Blaire turned against us and started staying out all hours with Susan. When we asked for an explanation, she ignored us. Things just started falling apart. Al and I didn't know what to do," said Gwen.

Since when did a twenty-four-year-old woman really tell her parents everything? For that matter, when did they live at home?

"Susan dressed sloppily," continued Gwen. "Her clothes were dirty and unkempt. She really liked the guys and talked of men wanting her." Gwen pulled herself up in a huff. "It had to be her imagination."

I asked Gwen if there was any particular guy Susan talked about. "Harley, I think his name was," said Blaire's mother. "When Blaire left with Susan, they went to live with him."

Gwen thought she had to explain Blaire's actions. "Blaire wanted a sister badly, and for some reason, which I can't understand, she and Susan hit it off.

"The two girls were inseparable. In time, Blaire changed. For the first time, Al and I felt left out of her life." Then, according to Gwen, Blaire started talking about finding her real mother. Gwen blamed Blaire's interest on Susan.

"But what information did Susan have about the whereabouts of her real mother? I thought that kind of thing was protected by law," I said. If it was that easy to find her biological mother, Blaire could have done it any time. But she didn't," I reasoned.

"Until that girl came here," Gwen said. "Then, when Susan stole the money......."

My ears perked up.

Gwen shook her head. "We could never prove it, of course. I kept money in a brown jar in one of the cupboards. I would try every week to save some cash from the groceries. Then, if there was any added expense, or if we had a special occasion, I would take it from there."

"How much do you think Susan stole?" I asked.

"I know I had at least a hundred dollars in the jar. I was saving up for a new dress."

"Did you confront Susan?"

Gwen shook her head. "I didn't want to make a scene. Besides, I know she would have denied it. "Gwen said then she and Al hired a private detective

The woman had to save grocery money to buy a new dress, but they hired an investigator. I waited for what may come next.

"He found out Susan was into drugs. The first thing we thought of when the money was missing was that Susan would buy drugs, and our Blaire would try them. And, then, there were other brushes with the law," Gwen said.

"Well, when we got the report from the investigator, we showed it to Blaire, hoping she would understand maybe she had been naive about Susan," explained Gwen.

"And?"

Gwen sat up straighter on the couch. "Blaire was angry and said we were wrong to do what we did. She stormed out of the house. Blaire wouldn't speak to us the next couple of days, and then she and Susan took off."

"Is that when they went to Harley's?" I asked.

"Susan left first in the middle of the night. Didn't even thank us for letting her stay here," Gwen said indignantly. "We breathed a sigh of relief, though. We thought that would be the end of it. Then Blaire left a couple of days later." The woman deflated as a balloon. "She left us a note. She said she and Susan were going to find their biological mother. She hoped we would eventually understand. That was the last contact we had with her." The woman crumbled in front of me again but after a few minutes continued. "The investigator told Al and me that Blaire and Susan were staying on the other side of Quincy. It was a dive.

"I went to see Blaire. This was no time for pride."

Gwen told me Susan answered the door and took delight in telling her Blaire didn't want to speak to her. Gwen went to the Quincy Sentinel, but her daughter made a scene, and the security guard had to escort her out. How humiliating, I thought.

"I'm sorry." I meant it.

"Another day, I waited until Blaire went to lunch. I knew she always went to the Burger King across the street from the newspaper."

It was getting late, and I wanted to get out of there before Blaire's father came home. I had what I needed, and the answers lay back in Sandy Ridge.

Gwen had told me that, according to the private detective, Susan had gotten a job as a newspaper reporter in Maine. She was my roommate. When I asked Gwen why both girls went to Sandy Ridge, she looked at me as if I should already know.

"Susan told Blaire their biological mother lived in Sandy Ridge.

Chapter 21

"Did Blaire tell you her biological mother's name?" I asked, crossing my fingers.

"We think Susan told Blaire, but Blaire wouldn't tell us," said Gwen. "By this time, our daughter thought we were the enemy." Her eyes became moist. It was time to leave. My legs were cramped, and I was chilled. My stomach growled loudly. Blaire's mother looked startled.

"I'm sorry," I said, looking at my watch. It was seven-thirty

Gwen put on the lamp at a nearby table. "It's getting cold here. I'll check the thermostat.

The woman walked me to the door. I thanked her for the time and told her I would like to stay in touch. Gwen hugged me. Her spontaneous display of affection touched me. Blaire had probably received many such hugs. I was envious. There hadn't been much of that in my family.

Susan said her mother was a writer, and that's what she wanted to be.

"Do you know what kind of a writer her mother was?" Gwen smiled. 'She said the woman was a reporter."

"In Sandy Ridge?" I asked. That rocked me. "There's only one newspaper in Sandy Ridge. The Courier, the one I worked at." This woman must be mistaken.

"That must be the one, then," Gwen said with conviction. I asked her if she had told the Sandy Ridge Police. The woman nodded. Hall hadn't indicated any of this to me.

She snapped on the outside light, and I walked to my car, turning back once to wave at her standing in the doorway. Where was Blaire's father? It's kind of late for him to be out if he's so concerned about his wife.

Did Gwen know what she was talking about? It could be another town nearby, for all I knew, and Gwen thought it was Sandy Ridge. I thought of all the women at The Courier that could have a daughter Blaire and Susan's age. How many were there?

First things first. Now, which way to get out of here and back to the hotel?

It appeared Gwen would stay in the doorway until I left, so I started my car and proceeded out to the street. A right onto the main drag, and I recognized landmarks, a convenience store and a beautiful home with a Century 21 sign in front.

Peanuts would help these hunger pangs until I got to a restaurant to eat dinner. I ran into a small store. My mind was on overdrive with what I had found out, but I would sort it out later at dinner.

The peanuts were so good I went back to get another package. Surprisingly, I found my way back to the hotel. It had to be the peanuts. They made me alert and focused.

Once inside my room, I called down to the desk and said I would be checking out in the morning. They would leave my bill under the door sometime during the evening. Looking at the desk in front of me, I spied an advertisement for the hotel's cafe. I opted to try it.

The cafe was called Tres Joli. The ceilings had crystal chandeliers. The walls were a black fabric with splashes of pastels running through it. This must be what a brothel in France looks like.

The tables were set with light pink tablecloths and fancy silverware with gold rims. Prices were high, and I hoped my credit card would go through one more time. It did.

One should order French onion soup in a place like this, but I ordered garden vegetables. Then I treated myself to a sirloin steak, baked potato and salad. The food melted in my mouth. I took out my notebook and wrote down the information Gwen had given me.

It sounded like Susan had been my roommate. Susan had come to Sandy Ridge to find her biological mother. Blaire had followed, but why had the girls fought before leaving Quincy?

My mother always told me to finish my meals. I am still held by that philosophy. Of course, it doesn't hurt that it's delicious. The meat was medium rare, cooked to perfection. I filled the potato with butter and sour cream. I chose low-cal dressing for the salad. I ate heartily and looked at my notes.

"Are you eating dessert tonight?" asked the waiter, bringing over a cart filled with gooey, tantalizing treats.

I looked at them longingly and decided on the peanut butter supreme. I know, don't say it!

"Could you bring decaf coffee and the check too?" The peanut butter supreme was all one could imagine. Delicious vanilla ice cream with caramel and peanut sauce. There was lots of real whipped cream on top with more peanuts. I saw my disease of compulsive overeating in full bloom as I downed the dessert with gusto. I thought of lapping the dish but knew that would be tacky.

The waiter was efficient and personable, so I left him a good tip. On the way out of the cafe, I noticed some sharp guys around the bar. Thoughts of Ted came to mind. I would be glad to go home. But would Ted be glad to see me after our last encounter?

You're pathetic, Allison. Ted's the one who screwed up. He's the one who got drunk and tried to get lucky. He'll be lucky if you forgive him. But I knew I would.

Once in my room, I undressed, laid some clothes out for the next day, packed the things I wouldn't need and set the alarm for seven in the morning. I got into bed and fell asleep immediately, but not for long. I woke up around two o'clock in the morning. My body was hot and sweaty. Had I gotten the flu shot? No. I'd been out of town when the Board of Health had come to The Courier.

I found headache medicine in my travel case and climbed back into bed, hoping I would feel better in the morning. When the alarm went off, I groggily hit the snooze button. I suspected I had a fever and lay there contemplating my choices. There were none.

When the alarm went off again, I got up and looked in the mirror. It was not good news. My hairline was soaked with sweat, and my eyes were glassy. Checkout was at eleven a.m. I called down to the desk and asked for a later checkout, then hit the sheets.

At nine-thirty, the phone rang. The caller wanted Ellen. I told him she wasn't in my room. He apologized. I looked in the mirror. My face looked better, and my body didn't ache. I grabbed my clothes, went into the shower, packed and left.

There was a short line at the front desk. When it was my turn, I passed her my bill, and she asked if I wanted it all on VISA. That sounded good to me, with only a couple of bucks in my purse. She thanked me for staying at the Madison.

The undercover garage where I had left my car could be reached directly from the side entrance. I had validated my parking ticket at the front desk, so there was no charge.

It was a sunny day. I put my bag in the trunk of my car and walked the short distance to a pharmacy. The druggist listened and suggested stronger nonprescription medicine, and if I didn't feel better, to contact my physician when I got home.

I bought some gum and peanuts while I was at it and washed the gross medicine down with a candy bar. Now, let's get home, I thought.

The ride out of Quincy was easier than coming in. There was no traffic going through Boston at noontime on a weekday. Everybody was working or having lunch. Thoughts of another meal tantalized me as I drove north to Maine, but I decided I wasn't going to stop until I got to my condo. I ate the peanuts, then chewed on the gum. With the exception of a good night of sex, what more could anyone ask for?

I made the trip in good time and was glad when I saw the first familiar sights of Sandy Ridge. My condo was intact. So was Muffy. When I go away, I have Mrs. Thompson next door come in and feed Muffy.

The cat was glad to see me. "Muffy," I laughed, "let me get my things unpacked. I can't move with you rubbing against my legs." I gave up and sat down. Muffy jumped up in my lap. "Sweet Muffy, what are we going to do next?" The cat cocked her head.

How was I going to find Blaire and Susan's mother? If she did work for The Courier like Gwen Nugent thought, how was I going to find her?

"Do you think I can get my old job back," I asked Muffy. The cat stared at me with her blue-green eyes, curled up in my lap and took a snooze.

That seemed like a good idea. I sat back in the recliner and closed my eyes.

Chapter 22

I hate taking naps usually because when I wake up, I'm groggy and can't seem to get myself together. I slept two hours, Muffy was still on my lap, and I felt drunk.

Staggering to the kitchen, I fixed myself some coffee and returned to the recliner. "Muffy, let's call it a night."

She lifted her head, looked at me and stretched, returning to her original position.

It was nine o'clock. It was well past dinner time.

What was I going to eat?

A look and a smell in the fridge told me something was foul. Ugh. I started chucking food that had spoiled while I was away. I tied the trash up for the morning and decided to call for Chinese takeout.

Waiting for the delivery, I unpacked.

It was then I noticed the phone blinking. I had deleted all calls from Mother and Joan when I was on the road. I didn't want to talk with them now. My relationship with my family was so complicated, and I wasn't sure how to react to them. I knew I didn't want to act the same with them. After being with

Gwen and Al and seeing their love for Blaire, no matter what, I knew I didn't want to act the same with my family as I had in the past.

After being with Gwen and Al, with their circumstances, I wanted some time alone to figure out my part in my family's screwed-up life and change it.

Deleting every message, I almost missed it. Ted's deep voice filled the room. "I acted like an ass. Can we talk?"

Hmm. Interesting. No! I needed time away from everybody right now.

I gave the delivery boy an extra tip when he brought my chicken wings, pork fried rice, crab Rangoon and chicken chow Mein.

Muffy kept weaving in and out of my feet. "I'm going to trip on you," I warned. The food was hot and delicious. I got a full plate, turned the TV on and sat back to enjoy. Muffy jumped up to sit beside me and to get whatever I dropped.

"Your fickle cat," I told her. "You're just after my chicken." Muffy has a sweet face, and she looked up at me now as if to say, "You better believe it.'" I gave her a piece of chicken.

I realized my next step was to talk with Hall and fill him in on what I learned on my trip. The next day, I called, telling the Police Chief briefly about my trip but asking to come in to see him sometime that day. He was checking his calendar when my call waiting buzzed/. For some reason, I took it automatically. It was Joan. Through tears, she told me Mother was in the hospital. EMTs just took her. "They think she had a stroke but won't know until doctors check her out."

"When did this happen?"

"Today. If you called me back, you'd know she hasn't been feeling well, and I've been worried about her. Where the hell have you been? Mother's been worried sick about you."

"Mother, worried about me?" I couldn't believe it.

"If you didn't only think of yourself all the time, maybe you would realize she loves you," said Joan. "She doesn't know how to express her feelings, but I've never seen her so worried, calling you every day, wondering where you are."

"I'll leave right now for the hospital. Are you there now?"

"Yes. She's in the ER but will be going up to Intensive Care."

When I hung up, I heard Hall on the other line. "What happened?" he asked. I told him and he said to call him or come into the station when things quieted down. "I'm sorry about your mother," he added.

I grabbed my purse, drove at rapid speed to the hospital a mile away and ran into the Emergency Room. Joan met me at the door. She saw my face.

"Calm down before you go in and see Mother. You're white." I sat down, Joan beside me.

"Take some slow, deep breaths," my sister directed.

"Is it bad?" I asked.

Joan shook her head. "They haven't said. I don't think they know yet, but doctors want her in the ICU now until they find out." My sister said she had gone over to Mother's to see how she was that morning. She complained of her face being numb. Joan knew to call EMT s immediately. Mother was on a respirator, so she couldn't talk but could hear us. I started crying.

"We don't want to get Mother upset, so let's just see what happens. If she sees you've been crying, she'll suspect the worst," said Joan. I nodded and followed Joan into my Mother's room. She was sleeping. We both sat on chairs next to her bed. Joan looked at her watch.

"It's time to pick up Timmy," she said.

"I'll stay," I told her. "Get Timmy from the playgroup and go home. Rest while Timmy takes his nap. I'll call you when she wakes up."

My sister hesitated, then leaned over to whisper. "Don't say anything about the money, and don't say anything about Ronnie." I looked at her.

"I'll explain later," Joan said, heading toward the door.

My mother was white, and her eyes were closed, but that didn't necessarily mean she was asleep. I took her hand and spoke quietly to her, saying that she was alright and that everything was going to be OK.

"I'm sorry about going away and not wanting to talk to you. I was in Quincy and was trying to find out who my roommate was. I'm sorry about being so selfish, only thinking about my situation. I'm only trying to get my job back. But I never thought you would get sick and end up in the hospital." I told her I loved her and would stay with her. I told her how Joan had to get Timmy and then would have to bring him home for his nap. "She said she'll be back later on. Please don't worry about anything. Just get well.

I'll stay here if you need anything." A tear dropped from my eyes to the hand I was holding. I didn't even know I was crying. My mother opened her eyes and caressed my cheek with her hand. I laid my head on the sheets. She put her hand on my hair.

I fell asleep but woke up when I heard a nurse coming in to check my mother's vitals.

"Looks like you both are having a good nap," she smiled.

My mother wasn't moving, and I realized she was still asleep.

"Is she alright?" I asked.

The nurse told me she had just given my mother something to sleep, and she would probably sleep through the night.

"How is she?" I asked.

"Every day we'll see her get stronger. She's in the right place."

Assured, I asked the nurse where the cafeteria was so I could get a cup of coffee. She directed me. I got a large espresso and returned to the chair at my mother's bedside.

Chapter 23

In the days that followed, I didn't call Ted. Let him stew. I thought about what my sister said and decided she could be right. Admitting this was hard, but it was selfish of me just to take off and tell nobody where I was going. I had a hair across my ass about Ronnie and Mother. If I was honest with myself, I did miss her while I was gone, and then I found out that Mother was in the ICU. I was scared I was going to lose her, and we would never have the chance to really get to know each other instead of always finding fault with what she did. Maybe, I mused, I'm jealous Mother can attract a guy ten years younger than her and keep him happy while I'm still looking for a guy that will treat me right. Ted and I weren't going anywhere. He only wanted my booze, my cable and once boozed up, my body. It's not a great endorsement for a husband to love and cherish me.

But not calling him didn't mean I wasn't thinking of him and trying to convince myself I should call him. Maybe I should join a dating site on the Internet.

A month went by. My Mother was improving and was moved down to a regular room. I visited daily, sending out resumes for a job in between visits to the hospital. And I did join a dating site on the Web called

"True Love." What the heck, you never know. Some guys sent me a smile, but their profile didn't send a flutter in my heart if you know what I mean.

Mother and I were getting along very well, and I needed to concentrate on that now. My heart did belong to Ted. I had always gone for the unapproachable, aloof, good-looking guys, and it looked like I wasn't changing my taste in men. That would have to be the next change I must make in my life, but I wasn't sure I wanted to do that.

Weeks became months, and somehow, I forgot about Ted. Mother was released from the hospital, and I spent a lot of time in her house. I hadn't seen Ronnie in several months since he chose to visit Mother's evenings when I wasn't there.

I was bringing her books I knew she liked, and now that she was home, Ronnie, Mother and I actually talked enthusiastically about the upcoming health club. Joan could join us whenever she could, and my sister brought Timmy many times. We all knew Mother adored Timmy.

I found myself enjoying Ronnie's company and sensed I was changing my mind about him. He did love Mother, who's health was back to normal, and she and I were going out of our way to please each other.

The weather was changing now, and soon, cold weather would be here. I now wore a coat where ever I went, and soon snow was in the forecast. My money was low, but I still persevered with resumes, hoping I would get a job writing. Meanwhile, the economy took a downturn, and jobs were drying up.

Thanksgiving would soon be here. I did some shopping got Mother a hostess gift as she insisted on cooking for the holidays. Ronnie had been doing more of the cooking since Mother came home, so he said he'd been in charge, which appeared to be OK with Mother.

Coming home one evening after shopping, it just didn't seem possible that someone would be waiting on the steps outside my apartment until I climbed the stairs and saw him. I almost didn't recognize him. Ted had grown a beard and a mustache. He was sitting on the highest step, waiting for me.

"About time you got home," he teased, smiling.

"Ted, what are you doing here?"

"I've called you several times, and you're ignoring me, so I thought I'd come over to see if you had moved."

He stood up as I walked past him. We were so close. I thought for sure Ted might be able to hear my beating heart.

"You want to come in?"

"Sure," he said.

I willed him to move away from me so I could breathe. But he didn't. I turned around to shut the door, and he took me in his arms and kissed me, his tongue reaching into my mouth, my tongue responding to his passion.

We moved into my bedroom, dropping clothes along the way, needing to be as close to the other's body as we could.

Our lovemaking was urgent and intense. I was in ecstasy, and I don't mean the drug, because I didn't need any - drugs, that is. Finally, exhausted, we slept, curled in each other's arms.

It was nine-thirty the next morning that I stirred and opened my eyes. It seemed to me I had been dreaming, but every muscle ache as if from an aerobic workout. Ted had left a note on my end table.

"See you tonight." He had made a heart and signed his name.

Last night had happened. It wasn't a dream or a figment of my overactive libido. The note proved it. I was delirious. Ted had signed the note "love." Isn't that what a heart means?

I danced out into the kitchen and made coffee and breakfast. It was an abstinent breakfast. I would lose weight now like never before. Thoughts of last night's passion came to mind. Thank goodness it had been dark. Ted hadn't seen my bulges. I would exercise. I would go to diet group meetings like never before.

The phone rang. I answered it.

"Allison, darling, where have you been?"

"Are you alright?"

"Yes, yes, I'm fine, don't worry. It's just that it's been a couple of days, and I hoped everything was OK. You've spoiled me, coming over to see me every day."

"Mother, I got home late last night and slept in this morning. You were first on my list to call, however."

"So why don't you come over for lunch today, and I'll show you the prints for the health club.

"Mother, I'd love to, but I just had breakfast."

"That's fine," she replied. "Tell me when you can come over, and we'll eat then."

Mother wasn't going to let me get away. "How about one thirty?" I relented.

"Sounds good. You'll love the prints for the health club. We've gotten a good builder, and plans are going ahead smoothly. It's exciting."

When I hung up, I called Joan.

"Mother invited me for lunch at her place. Can you join us? Please say you'll come."

"She's in high gear about the health club now that she has the money, "said Joan.

"Where did she get the cash?"

"Mother took a second mortgage on the house," Joan replied.

I sucked in my breath. Joan hurried on. "Let her do what she wants."

"What has Ronnie done?" I asked, irritated. "Does he have a place to mortgage?"

"He sold his car."

"His BMW?" That was a surprise. Thoughts of Ronnie not having his precious toy to prance around town amused me. He acted so superior in his fire engine red BMW with black seats.

Joan cleared her throat. She always did that before she gave me hell. I waited.

"Allison, why don't you stay out of this? Mother knows how you feel about her and Ronnie. You've told her many times. You told me about the Nugent's and how they'd give anything to have their daughter back to reconcile their differences. They don't have that chance. You do. Think about that today when you're over Mother's and try to be civil. She was really upset when you left town, and she didn't know where you were. Ronnie was too. Mother was calling Ted. It was bedlam.

"This will get you madder at me, but I like Ronnie. So does Doug. And Ronnie's good to Timmy. Mother is happy being with Ronnie. Won't you try to understand her, please," she continued on a roll. "Timmy and I will come over later."

"Benedict Arnold." Joan laughed.

We rang off. I mulled over what Joan had said, then called my diet club sponsor. We talked about Mother and Ronnie, my feelings about them and how my reaction to circumstances hadn't worked up until now. We discussed what Joan had said.

She listened and told me to stay abstinent with the food no matter what. The rest would become clear to me.

When we rang off, I sat at the kitchen table for a while. Finally, noticing the time, I got dressed and went to my Mother's. On the way, I rehashed what Joan and my food sponsor had said.

I was totally different in disposition than Mother. Even physically - I was blond, had light skin, she was dark. When my Father drank, I blamed my Mother. If she was different, then my Father wouldn't have taken to the bottle. Father had died of Cancer, but in my heart, I had blamed Mother for his deterioration. Mother had gravitated towards Joan. She was more pliable and relented when Mother was arguing.

Mother was different. But was it wrong? I asked my Higher Power for patience and tolerance as I parked in front of our family home. I asked my Higher Power to bring back my utopic feelings about last night and remember how happy I was that Mother was feeling better.

CHAPTER 24

Mother opened the door immediately as if she was waiting for me and hugged me profusely.

"I'm so glad you're home."

"Thanks, it's good to be home," I said with a smile, warming to her attention.

We walked into the living room. Mother had changed the furniture again. The couch was against the wall, and several chairs were on the opposite wall. A loveseat and recliner I didn't recognize complimented the grouping.

"I have lunch already," Mother chirped. "We'll eat in the dining room."

She led the way. We went into the kitchen and tossed the salad. Mother had prepared grilled chicken to put on top. There were sliced onions and pepperonis to spice up the salad. It was an abstinent lunch for me, complete with a Balsamic vinegar-type salad dressing she knows is my favorite.

Lunch was amiable enough. Mother wanted to know where I had gone, and I told her I was working on an article to freelance. I realized then that with her being in the hospital and the many months of her recovery, my trip to Quincy had never been discussed. Nobody really had asked me about it, and when I heard Mother was sick, my trip had been of no importance.

My Mother accepted my answer but asked me if I was running out of money, what with "being out of work and all."

"Why? Are you giving any away?" As soon as the words were out, I regretted them. Mother pretended not to notice. "Because if you are, you can always come to me." Mother hesitated and looked at me. She was set to say something but thought better of it.

"How's the salad," she asked.

"Delicious."

"Good. After lunch, I'll show you the prints of the health club." She smiled excitedly. "It's going to be a hit in Sandy Ridge. All of my friends say it's about time."

"Yes, Sandy Ridge does need a health club," I said, wanting to match her enthusiasm.

My Mother was exuberant. She looked so happy. Remembering last night and early this morning, I could identify.

After we finished lunch and put the dishes in the dishwasher, Mother led me to the "Library," as she calls it. The circumstances today were better than the last time when Mother had asked me to cash in my CDs so she and Ronnie could use the money for the health club. Thoughts of my storming out of the house that day came back.

Mother had several large tables side by side. She went to a large closet and took out rolls of white prints. Mother laid out the heavy sheets. They rolled up. I looked around and found some heavy objects to act as paperweights. Both Mother and I stood looking down at the drawings. She smiled at them while I tried to focus on what was in front of me.

Mother pointed out various features. The health club would be on one level, with the main area where the exercise machines would be located. The room would have glass walls so everyone could see their beautiful bodies grunt and sweat. There were going to be twenty treadmills, seven stationary bikes, and fifty assorted presses.

According to the drawings, there would be a second floor for babysitting. The code at the top of the prints was different colors - yellow for the babysitting rooms, gray for the exercise rooms, and white for special rooms for the aerobics and yoga classes.

Green would be the massage room. Pink was for women's locker rooms, and blue for men.

Cute.

"This is a big undertaking," I told my Mother. "It's grand, but it will cost a great deal of money," I said.

"That's for sure," Mother agreed.

"You have your heart set on this, but at your age, should you be doing this?" I asked.

Oops!

"Not that you're old Mother. That's not what I meant. It's just that you haven't done anything like this before, and with you being sick……….."

To my surprise, Mother laughed. She then grew serious and locked eyes with me.

"I know exactly what you meant." She shrugged. "It doesn't matter. Ronnie and I are going ahead with the club. We have a good feeling about it. You shouldn't be so full of fear at your age, Allison."

I reached over and hugged Mother. "Maybe so. Good luck with it." What could I say? You're an old fool. Grow up. Mother always got what she wanted from as far back as I could remember. She had made up her mind about this, and she was going to have it. We were saved from further discussion by the sound of a key in the lock and Joan and Timmy in the doorway.

"We're in the library," Mother called.

Timmy ran in. Mother bent down to hug the boy. "Didn't I tell you not to run, Timmy?" my sister chided.

"Leave him alone," Mother retorted. "He's the only one that runs like that to see me anymore."

"How is everybody?" Joan inquired, looking at me.

Mother picked up Timmy and came over to me. She put her arm around me. She gave me a half hug.

"I'm so glad to have my girl back."

I gave an exaggerated smirk. "You're never going to get rid of me." Turning my attention to Timmy, I extended my arms. "Don't I get any hugs anymore?" He quickly obliged. "Wow, you're getting heavy."

Mother wanted to show Joan the prints, so I entertained Timmy. He sat on my lap on the couch in the living room, and we talked about his preschool and friends he had over at his house recently.

All talked out, he jumped down and turned on the TV, surfing the channels until he found cartoons, then climbed back up to cuddle.

Apparently, I had been saved from a longer presentation on the health club than Joan. There is just so much of Scooby-Doo one can watch, however, if you know what I mean. My head jerked as I must have nodded off to sleep, and I caught myself. Timmy had fallen asleep. He looked so peaceful, and he tore at my heartstrings. I laid him down, put a pillow under his head, and he turned over to go into deeper slumber.

I went into the library. "Hey, are you girls coming out?"

They both looked uncomfortable. My eyes went to Joan. "We were talking about you," she said cheerfully. "You look good. But this is the first time you've disappeared like that, so Mother wanted to know if you told me more than you told her."

Mother looked sheepish.

"I told you what happened. It was research for a story that I hope will get me my job back."

"Why don't you try doing something else, dear," began Mother. It was an old record that was warped. The family had lost count of how many times Mother had suggested I get another line of work. She wanted her daughter to have a more prestigious job.

Before I could make a caustic remark, Joan interrupted. "Come here and look at these great prints."

"I've seen them. It's a big undertaking."

"Ronnie and I can do it." Mother then said that Joan could have a job as an aerobics instructor when the club opened. "You can too, Allison, if you lose some weight. By the way, are you still doing that "Program?"

I wondered whether I should tell Mother about the workout I got last night with Ted, but I vetoed the idea.

Joan put her arms around Mother and came over to me. "Let's go back into the living room and sit down. Timmy needs to wake up. Otherwise he'll be up all night."

As we were moving into the hall, we heard the front door open. Ronnie called out my Mother's name.

"Vera, are you home, hon?"

Mother did a power walk to the door. "Sweetie, come in and see the girls."

Joan and I looked at each other. Since when does "Sweetie" have a key?

Ronnie and Mother met at the top of the stairs and gave each other a long kiss. Both of us looked away. It's embarrassing to see your Mother score.

The lovebirds were really into it. Joan coughed, and they both looked at us. Mother blushed. Ronnie was nonplussed.

"Hi," he said.

"Hi yourself," I said, looking at Mother, who was still blushing. It was fascinating to watch.

We all moved into the living room again. They looked at us, then looked at each other. Mother blushed again. Her eyes sparkled. We sat down. Timmy woke up to the sound of our voices. He jumped up on my sister's lap. Ronnie came over and crouched before the boy. "How's my big fella?" he asked.

Timmy rubbed his eyes and moved closer to Joan. "He's still sleepy," she explained.

"I feel tired myself," Ronnie said, winking at us. "It's OK, champ, to take a nap during the day. I might have one this afternoon." He looked at my Mother. Did she blush again, or was it continual?

"Ronnie, sweetie, why don't you take Timmy to the kitchen and give him some of the cookies I baked this morning? You can have some, too," Mother joked. "And give him some milk to wash it down." She looked at us. "Do you want some?"

Both Joan and I declined. Mother was blushing again. Did she just have a dirty thought?

Mother waited until she heard Ronnie and Timmy in the kitchen, then she began.

"Girls, it's been almost two years since your Father died. It was hard living with your Father, with the alcohol and all. But he got sober towards the end, and we both had a glimpse of how it could have been."

We nodded.

"It was good at the end. Now I'm excited about the health club plans, and it's almost like I'm starting a new life."

"That's nice, Mother," Joan interjected.

What a brown nose, I thought. Where the heck was this conversation going?

Mother began to talk again, then paused. She toyed with a loose thread on her cardigan, then started to talk like an erupting volcano.

"Ronnie and I got married last week, and we hope you will be happy for us."

CHAPTER 25

My sister and I sat transfixed. Joan was the first to recover and went over to kiss Mother. "How wonderful. Doug and I hope you'll be very happy."

I heard the words but couldn't comprehend. Joan was her usual enthusiastic self. I could hear her in the background, but I couldn't move. Mother and Ronnie were married! Is this how he got her money? Was Mother a bigger fool than I thought? I sat there for what seemed like a long time. Mother was blushing over Joan's attention but loving it. Mother looked so happy. Please, God, let me be this happy sometime. Words my sponsor and Joan said to me earlier came to mind. They flashed through my head, and a thought came to mind. What could I possibly do to change this? Nothing.

I joined the group and kissed her on the cheek. "Congratulations."

"Girls, don't fuss so," Mother said, enjoying every minute.

"We'll have a party for you both," Joan said. "Now, let's sit down, and you tell us all about it."

Mother called Ronnie into the living room. She sat in the chair, and he sat on the armrest. They held hands. Mother continued to blush. Man, was this embarrassing. My stepdaddy was twenty years older than me.

Mother was aglow. She told us she and Ronnie had been going over the plans for the health club one evening with their lawyer. They were exuberant over the way things were working out. After the lawyer left, Ronnie turned to Mother. She had suggested they go out and celebrate. He suggested they celebrate by getting married.

They went to a JP in Portland. "Afterwards, we ate at a fast food joint and registered at a Motel 6," she laughed.

"When was this?" I asked.

"Last Tuesday," piped Ronnie. "It's been a honeymoon ever since." Ronnie bent over to kiss my Mother. Blush, blush. Hell, at this point, I was blushing.

My sister again reiterated how great their news was. "You must have a party. It will be over at my house. Mother, give me a list of all the people you'll want to invite. Ronnie, you include your friends and relatives too. Allison, invite your friends."

Joan was all wound up. This was her specialty, having parties. She loved giving them and was good at it.

"Mother, you and Ronnie talk about what date is good, and Allison and I will do the rest." How did I get into this?

Joan stared at me with a look that said, help me here.

I thought she was doing very well. I looked at my watch. "Gee, I hate to leave during all this excitement, but I have an appointment in ten minutes. I'll get together with Joan later, and we'll talk about the details."

Mother and Ronnie got up. "Don't get up. I'll see myself to the door." I hugged Mother and kissed her on the cheek. "I'm very happy for you both." Ronnie looked like he was going to hug me any minute. Instead I took his hands. "Congratulations, you got a great gal."

As I was going down the stairs, I heard Joan call, "I'll talk to you soon." I didn't doubt it.

Once in the car, I turned toward the police station. I wasn't going to think about what just happened and the fact my Mother was now married again.

I wanted to see Hall and see if there had been any new developments. I needed to tell him about my trip to Quincy. Something told me I shouldn't keep it to myself, although I had told Ted the night before. Thoughts of last night made me smile.

The police station parking lot was empty, so I swung into a visitor's space and proceeded into the building. I asked the dispatcher for the Chief. After a moment, his booming voice told me to come in.

"I hear you've been busy," said Hall. Geez, what else did Ted tell him?

I sat down. Hall asked me if I wanted coffee. "No, thanks."

Hall took a sip of his and looked out at me from his desk. "I met the Nugent's," I began.

Hall shook his head. "It's tough when I have to go to a relative's house after a victim's death, especially a violent one." He shook his head. "They're nice people."

"Yes, they are. So, you knew about Susan? How come I have to research these things myself?" I said. "If you knew, how come you didn't let me in on it?"

"Because I don't consult you on police business? I didn't know you were going to Quincy."

I told him once I saw him on the interview show on cable, I knew I had to check it out.

"Blaire, having a sister is news, Chief."

"No, it isn't. It helps the police with their case, but the police don't want every detail out in the press. If it's hushed up about Susan, maybe we'll have more of a chance to find her."

"Is that what you're doing? Trying to track her down?"

"That and other things," said Hall.

I leaned forward. "Let's work together on this, Chief. I lost my job, remember."

Allison, you're a newspaper reporter through and through. You think like one. You act like one. Don't kid me. When we crack this case, you'll be on the phone to some newspaper, probably The Courier, to break it and get your job back."

"But in the meantime, we can consolidate our ideas, and maybe something will crack."

"Talk," he said.

"First of all, what do you think about the boyfriend?"

"What boyfriend?"

I was getting exasperated with Hall. He looked amused.

"Darren Quill, Blaire's boyfriend."

Hall told me he interviewed him. "And Harley?" I asked.

"Yeah. The guy's a jerk, but he's not capable of murder. And the same goes for Peter Buell. Besides, I think Buell had a crush on Blaire. He didn't want to hurt her. Can you believe that dump they lived in?" asked Hall.

My thoughts went back to the run down, dilapidated, three family that Gwen had said Susan and Blaire lived in with Harley, Susan's supposed boyfriend. Boy, was he a sleaze! And, Peter Buell, a student who lost his job and could only afford to live in that dump. Buell told me the inside of the house was better than the outside. I took his word for it. I agreed with Hall about Buell. He appeared to be a nice guy and I did think he had a crush on Blaire.

I shrugged. "I can't believe Blaire would live there for a minute, but I know she followed Susan, and that's where Susan lived. Susan kept that place even though she had been living with the Nugents for a while.

Hall said that he didn't think Blaire was as happy living with her adoptive parents as they thought.

"How come?"

"Blaire accepted Susan's story pretty fast, don't you think? If you were Blaire, wouldn't you check on Susan's story?"

"How do we know?? Maybe Blaire was lonely. She knew she was adopted. Maybe the girl fantasized about finding her real mother all this time," I said. "And then, when Susan came, she saw her opportunity.

"Which brings us to finding the real mother," I continued. "The Nugent's said Susan told Blaire the bio mother is a writer for a newspaper in Sandy Ridge. The only

newspaper in town is The Courier."

"OK, you tell me. You worked there. Who could be the Mother?"

I threw up my hands. "She'd have to be in her late forties, early fifties. Maybe older. That's about every female there."

Hall stood up. We had come to an impasse. "Let me know what you're up to," the police chief said, leading me to the door and opening it.

"Susan could have been mistaken. It could have been another newspaper in the area," I said. "Are you still going to pursue the case?"

Hall shook his head. "I don't know. The trail is getting cold."

Stepping out the door, the sun shining on my face, I decided it was a good day for a walk to do some errands in the area. There was a department store down the street that sold everything. It was sheer joy to go there. If I wasn't eating compulsively, shopping was my next addiction. But today, in spite of the mystery of Blaire and Susan that hung over my head, I wanted to indulge in that compulsion.

I went back to the police station and asked the dispatcher if I could leave my car in the parking lot while I did some shopping. He agreed, and I took off with a bounce in my step.

I came upon a new shoe store. I could use a new pair of heels.

Looking in the window, I saw a pair that struck my fancy. I turned to go to the store when my reflection caught a familiar face across the street. I was delighted. "Lacey," I yelled.

"Lacy," I shouted louder. Those passing by stared at me. I ran to the curb and yelled again. I was delighted to see the face of my friend. I waited for a hole in the traffic and ran across the street. "Lacey, Lacey, wait up."

She was surprised. "Allison, what are you doing around here?"

I laughed. "It is out of the way from my condo, but I was visiting Police Chief Hall. How about you? Aren't you working today?" Lacey appeared at a loss for words.

"I bet Shaw is out today, and you took a longer lunch hour," I laughed.

She nodded. "I have been thinking about you," Lacey said. "How is everything?

Have you gotten a job?"

"No, not yet," I shrugged. "Can we go for coffee somewhere? I can catch you up on everything I've been doing."

Lacey looked undecided. "Com'on," I urged. "We can make it fast. It just seems so long since I've seen you."

She hesitated. I realized that I had caught her at a difficult moment.

"Sure," she said. There was a coffee shop right in front of us, so we went in there.

I asked a young girl who worked there if we could sit anywhere. She nodded and brought over menus. We both said we wanted coffee only, and she went to get it.

I asked Lacey about her father. She told me he had taken a turn for the worse and that last week had been bad.

"I'm sorry," I said.

"It comes and goes." Lacey looked sad. I asked her how The Courier was doing without me.

The coffee came. Lacey played with it, adding more sugar and cream.

"I thought you took your coffee black like me," I said.

The girl was startled. "I'm trying different ways to see if l like it better." I let that pass. The mood was unsettling, and I tried to figure out why.

When you don't see someone for a week or two after being so friendly, I guess it's awkward.

I told her about going to Quincy and meeting Blaire's parents. I told her about Blaire having a sister.

She looked at her watch several times. I was keeping her from work. "Listen, why don't we get together some night this week and catch up? I want to get your ideas about this. Plus, working at The Courier longer than I have, you can help me unravel what I heard. I know you have to get back to work."

"That would be better," said Lacey. She rose. I took one more sip of my coffee, and we both walked outside.

"Listen, I'll call you," I said.

"It's good to see you, Allison. I have to run, but let's get together soon."

We parted. I continued to the department store. Lacey, in the other direction.

"Isn't the Courier back this way?" I asked.

"Oh, yeah." Her car was in front of the coffee shop. "Do you want a ride?" she asked me.

"No, it's such a beautiful day. I feel like walking."

We said our goodbyes again, and I headed down the street. Lacey isn't herself today, I thought. It must be because of her father being ill.

Walking down the street, so many things came to mind I had wanted to share with Lacey. I wanted to tell her about Ted and meeting the Nugent's. I hadn't even gotten to the part about Susan. I realized I had missed seeing Lacey.

The department store was crowded. I bought a new pink cardigan, a white blouse and a pink floral skirt for tonight when Ted came over. I felt great. My food had been excellent so far today, and my mood was light.

I called my sponsor when I got home to tell her about my Mother. We talked about the day. I felt proud of how I had handled the afternoon at her house. She told me to accept my Mother's new husband and get on with my life. That sounded like a good idea. I gave her my food menu for the evening and rang off.

Muffy was meowing. There was nothing in her dish. I got a can of cat food out and gave it to her. She chowed down ravenously. Hmmm, maybe she's a compulsive overeater like myself.

Now that Muffy was taken care of, I got into the shower and washed my hair. After, I put lotion on and sprayed myself with cologne. The thought came to me that I should look to see if I had any messages. Ted might want to go out to dinner tonight.

The first message was Joan asking when I could get together with her to plan Mother's wedding party. Then, Mother's voice. She thanked me for coming over that afternoon, said she and Ronnie were very happy, and they hoped I wouldn't be a stranger.

I turned to put on the skirt I had bought that afternoon when I heard Ted's voice.

"Sorry, I can't make it tonight. Something important came up. I'll call you."

Chapter 26

I took the new skirt, rolled it up in a ball, and threw it across the room. I went into the kitchen and flung open the cupboards. All of a sudden, I was ravenous. I perused the shelves. I had the jar of peanut butter in my hand. I took a knife out of the drawer and got the crackers.

"Oh, what the hell. I got a spoon, scooped the peanut butter up and ate it, but I choked on the enormous amount in my mouth and quickly grabbed the diet soda from the refrigerator. Determined, I finished the peanut butter, finally taking crackers down from the cupboard and methodically spreading it on. After a while, I got the raisins down and started making faces on the crackers, popping them in my mouth like this was my last meal. I called my sponsor and talked to her for about an hour. We talked about Ted. I cried. She listened. At the end of our conversation, I hated myself for what I had done and decided to go to bed.

Waking the next morning, I looked in the mirror and started crying again. My body was swollen, my face bloated. I got my first cup of coffee and ran to the bathroom, barely making it. What goes in must come out. I went back to bed. Muff jumped up to be with me. I patted her. "Let's let the rest of the world go by today." And that's what we did.

Three days later, I got up, took a shower, dressed and went out for breakfast. A look in my purse told me I better stop at the ATM on the way. My bank balance told me I'd better get a job fast. I could charge my breakfast. I bought a newspaper and read the Help Wanted Section over a breakfast of two eggs, pancakes, sausages, toast, butter, and coffee. Scanning the newspaper, I saw an ad for a psychic. Hmm, maybe that's what I need. My sponsor told me to do something good for myself every day. The psychic might give me a lift. I wrote the address and telephone number down. When the waitress came back saying my charge card had declined, it got a little sticky.

"Damn, I paid that bill yesterday. You see, I've been out of town and just came back," I told the waitress. She looked sympathetic. After all, it could have happened.

"Do you have another charge card?" she asked hopefully.

"No." I opened my wallet to show her that I only had a few dollars and no other charge card.

"I'll have to call over the manager." The waitress left.

The manager was younger than the waitress. A guy would call her cute, I suppose. She had long, permed black hair all over her face. What happened to the days when waitresses had to wear hairnets? She was chewing gum. My waitress explained my plight. I reiterated my hard luck story. The manager's eyes never left mine, trying to assess whether she should believe my story. This was taking too much time, although I didn't know where I was going from here, literally or figuratively. The psychic could tell me that.

"Look," I said, "why don't I write you a check? You keep it until I come back with the cash. I have money at the bank, and I'll cash a check and come back with it. Then you can return my check, and everybody will be happy."

Curly wasn't too sure I wasn't pulling a fast one. I took out my checkbook. "Please," I implored. "I'm so awfully embarrassed about this. I'm good for the money." I started writing the check. Curly looked at the waitress. She shrugged her shoulders.

"OK," the manager agreed reluctantly.

"See, I'll even include a substantial tip for the trouble I've caused."

That got everyone's attention. Both looked at the size of the check. I had given my waitress a ten-dollar tip for a five-dollar meal. Oh, well!

By now, everyone in the restaurant was staring at me. I got up as poised as I could, thanked both girls profusely and left. Damn, I had left my newspaper behind. One glance into the windows of the restaurant told me I wouldn't go back to get it.

There are times in everyone's lives when they feel like they've reached the bottom.

As I sat in my car, I knew I had reached that bottom. No job, no money, no self-respect. I had shelter over my head, but for how long if I couldn't pay the mortgage? I started the car and headed for help. It was going to kill me, but there was no choice. It was true; our relationship was better, and I knew I did love her, but when you ask relatives for money, it can get sticky. But I had to swallow my pride.

Ten minutes later, I pulled up in front of Mother's. Her car was in the driveway, along with her new husband's.

"Allison, how wonderful of you to drop by. Come in," she said enthusiastically. "We were just having breakfast. Would you like something?"

"No thanks. I've had enough."

If my Mother thought that was an odd remark, she didn't bite. We went into the kitchen, and I got juice out of the fridge and sat down. Ronnie was buttering his English Muffins, and Mother was making eggs for the both of them.

"So, what brings you over here so early in the morning?" Mother asked. She put two eggs once over on Ronnie's plate. Mother saw me look at them. "Did you eat this morning?"

"Yes. I had a big breakfast," I said. The food was settling like dark clouds before a rain right now.

We made small talk. The health club was coming along. The talk was centered on the holidays.

"I don't want to even think about that right now," I said.

Mother looked at Ronnie and gave him a look to get lost.

"I think I'll take my breakfast into the den and watch the morning news." He got up.

"Thanks, Ronnie. I do need to talk to Mother alone."

There was an uncomfortable pause. I heard the Portland newscaster in the background. "Let's have it, Allison," said Mother, never one to mince words.

To my surprise, I started crying. Between sobs, I told her I needed money. She listened.

"Have you been trying to get a job?" she asked.

"There's nothing out there," I sobbed, hiccupping now. I do that when I cry.

"Stop crying," she demanded. Oh, oh.

I tried. I held my breath but to no avail. "I may need something to eat." She looked at me. "Just a little wedge of your English Muffin. That could stop my hiccups." Mother pushed the plate towards me.

"How is your program going?" she asked.

Ouch!

"One thing at a time, Mother," I said, not too happy how this was going.

"If you could give me a loan," I continued, "until I get on my feet." "How much of a loan?" she asked.

"A few thousand."

"Allison, all my money is tied up in the health club, you know that," she said. "I can let you have three thousand dollars, but after that, you'll have to cash in the CDs your father gave you. You know the ones, don't you? The ones you wouldn't let me have for the health club."

"You have every reason to be mad," I relented, "but things weren't going well at the time for me, and I knew that was my insurance should I lose my job."

"Why not use them now, then?" Mother asked.

"Mother, if you give me the three thousand, I will pay you back," I implored.

She went to the counter, took her checkbook out of her purse and wrote the check. "I know you'll pay me back. I just want you to find a good job and be happy." She sized me up.

"You've been gaining weight too, and I know that doesn't make you feel good." She came over to me, handed me the check and hugged me. "Allison, find a job, even if it's at a fast food place. On second thought, don't do that."

My face reddened. "Mother, must you always talk about my weight?"

"It's important for a young, single girl to keep her figure. And you're a beautiful girl, Allison." Talking to Mother was like talking to a wall. I kept thinking it would change, but insanity is doing the same thing over and over again.

I hugged her and thanked her for the money. "Should we set up a plan for repaying you the money?" I asked.

"Don't be sarcastic, Allison. Take the money, get a job and pay it back when you can."

"I will." I turned to leave. "Thanks for helping me. You may not believe it, but I appreciate it."

My Mother nodded.

Once in the car, I was so ashamed and embarrassed to stoop so low as to ask my Mother for anything. I started the car, drove to the bank, and put the money in my checking account with the exception of one hundred dollars. Then, I drove to the restaurant and paid my breakfast bill. The manager returned my check. I tore it up. She looked at me expectantly. The tip! I had forgotten to include it in the check. I reached into my wallet, took a ten out and gave it to her. "Sorry, I forgot." If looks could kill.........

I was going to go home, but as I got into the car, the scrap paper with the psychic's name and telephone number fell out on the seat. I called her. The friendly voice on the other line told me to come over right away. What the hell! Things couldn't get any worse. My life was messed up; I needed a job first to bring in some income. But where?

Could the tarot cards have the answer?

The street was in an older section of Sandy Ridge but not far away. I passed the beach on the way. Young people were playing volleyball over a net. They appeared carefree and innocent. I wanted to trade places with them. When did things change for me? I thought back to my encounters with Shaw. I was so sure Blaire Nugent, or whatever her name is, was blackmailing Shaw. Why hadn't I shut up? No, I had to save Shaw, even if he didn't want to be saved. Oh, to do things differently. The guy behind me honked me out of my trance. I took a left and saw Sadie's sign right in front of me. "SADIE, Physic Readings, Tarot Cards." Her telephone number was in bold letters.

The street was a line of former summer cottages converted into winter houses. The paint was peeling on most of them. Doors were falling off, and railings were broken. It gave me a creepy feeling to be around here. Should I go to this physic healer? Did I believe in it? I didn't believe in too much anymore. I parked and got out of the car, locking my car lest it not be there when I came out.

Up ahead, a woman walked briskly across the street. Something about her stature appeared familiar. She looked behind her, like someone might be following her. It took me a minute to recognize her, but when I did, I shrank back. It was Lacey. What was she doing here in this part of town? The woman had a wide-brimmed hat on. I did several double-takes, but yes, that was her. Maybe I was mistaken. We hadn't talked for a while. Every time I called her, I got her answering machine, and she never returned my calls. It was strange because I thought we were getting to be good friends.

Waiting until the woman got into the house, I walked up to the dwelling. Suppose she came out soon and found me? I wasn't doing anything wrong? Was she doing something wrong? Not Lacey. She was probably visiting some relatives. She never talked about her family, except her father, but maybe she had aunts and uncles in this part of town. She never mentioned any sisters or brothers, but that didn't mean she didn't have any.

Lacey had gone into eight, nine and ten Prescott Street. Which one had she gone into? And why? I stayed in my car for a couple of hours, waiting to see if Lacey came out. She didn't, so I left.

My first thought the next morning was that I needed to be with people, never mind lonely stakeouts; someone that I could have fun with, laugh with and be myself, but someone who approved of me. Images of the gang at the office came to mind. It was fun to see them. They all had been surprised I didn't have a job yet, but we took each other at face value, and it hadn't been awkward. If truth be known, the reason I was thinking of the gang at the office wasn't just so I could see them again. I needed to pump someone about Lacey, and since I'd only been at the newspaper three years, what I needed was a veteran reporter. Rose Collier came to mind. So, I called her.

She was happy to hear from me. Rose had sat next to me at The Courier, and although we hadn't gone out after work socially, we had shared our lives with each other. She was married, had four kids, and seven grandchildren, which she adored. Rose had also worked at The Courier before Shaw. She knew pretty much everything that went on at The Courier.

Of course, job prospects came up in our conversation. I told her I was freelancing and working on a story right now but hadn't wanted to say anything when we last saw each other.

"Do you have plans for lunch today?" I asked.

"No, I don't, and I'd love to see you, Allison."

"Good." We made plans to meet at a place at noon that has a great salad bar.

I was early. Rose was on time. We hugged each other.

"It's so good to see you," she said, smiling.

"Me too. I'm sorry we haven't kept in touch before now."

"I do miss you at the newspaper. It's good about the freelancing. You're a good reporter. You need to stay in the business."

"Thanks." I felt good about seeing Rose again. No matter what my problem had been, Rose had always given me good advice. She had always made me feel better, and she was working her magic on me again today.

The waitress came over, and we ordered soft drinks.

"They have a fabulous salad bar if you like, or we could order from the menu," I said.

"My daughter told me about their salad bar. Let's go over and see what it looks like," Rose suggested. We did, liked what we saw and told the waitress when she brought our drinks.

When we had satiated our hunger, I asked how things were at The Courier. Rose shrugged. "It's the same as when you were there. Nothing changes."

"Is Shaw his usual charming self?"

"We got a couple of new people, and they can't believe the tantrums Shaw has."

I laughed. "I guess nothing's changed"

Rose returned to the salad bar. I followed. As we were filling our plates again, I asked how Lacey was. "I used to see her, but I guess she's been busy," I fished.

"Lacey's another one I can't figure out. She seems moody."

The waitress came over and gave us another soft drink as we returned to our table.

"Good service here," Rose noted.

"Yes. I never found Lacey moody. How is her father? Maybe he's gotten worse."

"She doesn't share about how her father is. In all the years I've known Lacey, I've never been able to figure her out.

This was news to me because Lacey and I had always hit it off. So, I asked Rose what she meant.

My friend leaned into the table to talk softer. "I was very nice to her when she first came to work at The Courier, you know, trying to help her get acclimated to the job. She was so young, fresh out of high school." This information startled me.

"Lacey told me she's worked at The Courier for the last ten years," I said.

"Oh, yeah, she has. But I'm talking about the first time around."

"What do you mean, 'this time around?'"

Rose looked surprised. "I didn't think it was any secret about her leaving and coming back. People do that. She tried her hand at another newspaper, I guess, and after a while came back. I couldn't imagine why she wanted to work for Shaw again, but there's no accounting for why people do things."

I tried to hide my excitement. "Yes, who'd want to work for Shaw if you ever met him." We both laughed. "How long have you worked at The Courier, Rose, and how come you can stand him?" I asked.

She threw up her hands and laughed again. "That's a good question. I can't believe that I've got twenty-five years into retirement. As for working for Shaw, maybe I'm a glutton for punishment. I can't believe how fast the years go. But I am close to retirement, and some days, I'm happy about that."

"You don't look old enough to retire," I said.

"Thank you, but the newspaper has a good early retirement plan, so in three years, I can kiss it all goodbye. Joe wants me to spend more time with him since he's already retired, and I want to spend more time with my grandchildren, who live close by before they get older and don't want to be with me. You know how that is?" Rose smiled.

"When I spend time with my Joe, our children and grandchildren, who cares about Shaw or the newspaper? Although, in a way, I feel like we've grown old together."

I asked Rose what she meant.

Rose told me Shaw had come to The Courier a couple of years after she started. "In fact, I had a crush on him. He was good-looking and single. Of course, I was not going out with Joe at the time. I saw Shaw come up through the ranks. He started as a reporter, just like me. He got assistant editor, then editor eventually. Shaw worked hard. You had to give that to him. He's always been dedicated to the job. That's why I think he never married."

"Did he ever ask you out?"

"We did go out once or twice, but nothing came of it." Rose smiled. "Boy, was he a catch! I was in heaven. He had such dreams."

"Dreams?"

"Of going to the New York Times, ya know, really making it in the newspaper business."

My head was swarming with questions, but I didn't want to appear too eager.

"Do you suppose that's why Shaw's so grouchy?" I asked.

"It's a shame he never married," Rose said. I nodded in sympathy. "It takes a woman to mold a man if you know what I mean," she said.

"Did any other girls at the newspaper get the chance? To date, Shaw, that 1s. I mean, when he was younger?"

Rose looked at me and laughed. "How did we get on this line of conversation? Believe it or not, I don't like to gossip."

"Nor I, but talking about Shaw gives me a little bit of understanding about how he was because I want to understand him and why he acted the way he did when he fired me. I really like Shaw and was desolate when that happened."

"I told him he was acting like a jerk." Rose patted my hand.

"You said that to him?" I laughed, visualizing Rose doing that.

She smiled. "I can get away with things like that with him since we go back so far."

"What did he say?"

"He said, 'Rosie, stay out of this.' "The waitress came over and asked if we wanted coffee or dessert. We declined. She left the bill on the table.

"That was delicious. We have to do this more often, Allison."

We figured out the bill, left a good tip and stood up. Rose hugged me, and we walked out. I was running out of time.

"Just for curiosity, who else in the newsroom got a chance to date Shaw in the old days?"

"Why are you so curious anyway, Allison? Who cares?"

"Nosy, I guess. It's hard to picture Shaw making out or hitting on anyone when you think of how he is now."

Rose came closer to me and talked in a whisper. "He dated all the single young women in the newspaper. He didn't care if his personal and business relationships intertwined. He loved them and left them. I did feel sorry for Lacey, though. She really loved him. I think that's why she left after he moved on to someone else."

Did this shed any light on anything? I decided to table it for now and warmly said goodbye to Rose. She appeared more reserved, and I quickly assured her that anything she had told me was confidential. Rose seemed to relax at that.

"We must do this again soon," I said, kissing her on the cheek.

"Yes, we will." My friend didn't register the same enthusiasm as me.

When I got home, I let Muffy out on my small porch. She jumps over to my neighbor's porch, which is identical to mine, and sometimes down to the first floor and then out to the yard. Early on, when she was a kitten and growing, I worried about her doing that, but she has survived, and I figure she knows what she's doing.

I sat on the porch and watched my cat. She was my constant companion.

Today, Muffy just seemed to want to purr as she moved between my legs. "Go play." Muffy looked at me and continued. That drives me crazy, but Muffy kept on doing it. I went in and sat on the couch. She did, too. My mind kept going back to what Rose had told me at lunch. Lacey and Shaw had been an item at one time. Funny, they never acted particularly friendly in the office. Why would Lacey want to come back to The Courier, especially if there was unrequited love between them? At least on Lacey's part, and why was Lacey visiting that triple-decker in the wrong part of town? Maybe I should ask her if, indeed, that was Lacey. Was there any doubt?

The clock on the entertainment center said it was three o'clock. If that person was true to habit, it would be a couple of hours until she appeared at the triple-decker.

A look in my wallet told me I'd better eat at home before going on the stakeout. If that woman was Lacey, would she recognize my car? Would she come over and ask what I was doing there? Couldn't I just be accidentally running into an old friend? I decided I'd worry about that when the time came. Grabbing an apple and a soft drink with my salad, I made tracks.

The traffic was in my favor, and I soon found the same spot from the day before, a little down the street from the house in question. Sitting in the car, tapping my fingers to easy listening music, was peaceful. The same people came by and went into the same houses, most slumped over, their shoulders heavy with worry about work, debt, or family. Maybe I didn't have it too hard, being single and all. Some looked my way, getting familiar with the car being in the same spot. Would one call the cops? What would I say? Rather than daydream, I should be thinking about plausible answers to those questions. I took a map of Sandy Ridge that was in my glove compartment and studied it. I could always say I was looking for an address in the area.

There she was! The woman, dressed in the same coat and hat, was locking her car door. Doing the same, I quickly walked across the street. Not too fast. I didn't want to draw attention. Staying on the grass so I wouldn't make noise, I approached her, wanting to catch her off guard. The figure in front of me had the same posture, height and build as Lacey. I was elated by this new development.

"Lacey, what are you doing around here?" I asked, grabbing the woman's shoulder. She jumped and started walking faster, clutching her purse. She thought I was trying to steal her purse. I kept pace with her and called her name out again. The woman turned to me, her eyes huge and round.

"Please, don't hurt me," she begged. "I don't have any money."

The voice wasn't Lacey's! The face resembled hers, but the woman was not Lacey.

"Please, I'm not going to harm you. I thought you were somebody I knew. Please forgive me."

"Do you usually sneak up on people you know?" she asked. The woman looked around. "Where are the cops when you need them?"

"Please, don't call the cops. It was an honest mistake. Listen, is there a place around here to get a cup of coffee? I would love to make this right somehow."

"Girlie, just leave me alone. Now get lost."

"Are you sure you're alright?" I asked.

"Yes, now go."

I apologized profusely a couple more times and got out of there.

Once in my car, I watched her go into the house. Strange how she looked like Lacey from the back, and her face, although different, was the same, if that made sense.

The woman looked back at me, staring as if giving me a voodoo hex. Just in case she was, I started the car and left, scolding myself for getting into something that could have been explosive.

You need to concentrate on getting a job, I told myself. I might never know what happened to the murdered girl or my former roommate, who called herself Blaire Nugent. There are cold cases that never get solved.

The following week was busy, with my sending out resumes to any newspaper within a radius of fifty miles. Friday Joan called and wanted me to go with her to Mother's.

"She invited us to lunch," Joan said. "Us?"

"She asked if 1 would call you. Why, what's the matter? Do you need a personal invitation?"

"Cute, Joan."

"Well?" my sister asked.

"What time are you going?"

"Timmy and I can pick you up in ten minutes," said Joan.

"Sounds good to me." After all, Mother had lent me money so I could pay my rent groceries, and live another day.

I changed out of my dungarees into a blouse and skirt with flats and went downstairs to wait for Joan and my nephew. She pulled up, and we made rapid time to our Mother's house. Timmy was in his car seat in the back. Joan was in a silly mood, telling her son corny jokes. It was fun seeing Joan and Timmy giggling, and I quickly joined in.

"You guys are silly," I said as we pulled up to Mother's house. She was waiting outside for us.

"How come you're out here?" I asked, getting out of the car.

"It's a nice day, and besides, I want to show everyone something."

An inner alarm went off in my mind. What was Mother up to now?

Mother picked up Timmy and gave him a hug and kisses. "How's my little boy?"

The boy's smile couldn't have been any bigger, and he returned her affection with glee. Joan smiled over at me. We could say what we wanted about Mother, but she loved her grandson immensely.

Our Mother didn't take us into the backyard to sit on the patio, which we usually do when it's warm as today. Instead, we stood outside, Mother showing us the newest flowers she had planted along the pathway from the house to the garage. When we had exhausted that, Mother told Timmy she had a surprise for him. He was delighted. Mother put him down and, holding his hand, led us to the backyard. I couldn't believe my eyes. Timmy was jumping up and down. Joan just stared; her mouth open. Mother chuckled over our reactions.

In front of us, where the backyard had been, was a huge Hollywood-type swimming pool, complete with a wide deck, two diving boards and water that reminded me of Ted's eyes.

"Isn't it wonderful?" Mother asked.

"Can I go in? Can I go in?" Timmy was shouting. Joan was trying to tell him he didn't have a bathing suit.

"I have one Timmy can use," Mother chimed in. "I just bought it for him."

"We have to get him a life jacket or water wings," Joan explained.

"I have those too," Mother said. "I bought everything for my little boy so he could go into the water and have some fun."

Timmy looked up at Joan, his eyes huge saucers of hope.

Joan looked at me. I gave her a look that said leave me out of this. My sister was aggravated. "Mother, why did you buy this?"

"Because I wanted to." She was defensive now. "Ronnie loves to swim, and he's going to teach me."

Mother bent down to Timmy. "Today, why don't we just sit by the pool under the umbrella table until your mother gets used to the surprise."

Joan glared at me. I wasn't getting into this. We sat down, or at least I did. Timmy ran to the edge of the pool, and Joan ran after him. Mother went in to get lunch. Might as well help her.

Lunch was a salad for me, tuna sandwiches and peanut butter and jelly for Timmy.

"You're going to have to put up a fence," I told Mother.

"I have someone coming tomorrow," she replied, putting salad on her plate.

The meal was delicious, but Timmy wouldn't sit down for his peanut butter and jelly sandwich. He was running from one end of the pool to the other with Joan in pursuit. She finally grabbed him and came back to the table.

"Mother, I wish you had told me about the pool, " she began.

The woman looked at her daughter. "I told you, everything he needs is in the house. Why don't you let him have some fun?

Timmy started begging. Please, Mom, please, please, please."

I ate my salad in silence. This was new. It was usually my Mother and I that were going at it. On some level, I was enjoying it.

For years, I tried to analyze my relationship with my Mother and even went to short-term counseling. My therapist had said I needed to accept her the way she was, but most importantly, I was to accept myself. But, somehow, my Mother and I always needed to give each other jabs. I made comments about Ronnie and their relationship, and she gave me a hard time about my weight. Joan stood by patiently running interference. So, today, seeing Joan frustrated with Mother kind of amused me.

Seeing Timmy so excited about the pool, I knew Joan would give in, and in the end, she relented, bringing her son into the house. Timmy put his new swim trunks on with his life preserver. My sister was furious but tried to conceal it as best she could. Mother changed and went into the pool with him. Joan, all the time, warning Timmy to stay at the shallow end.

My sister finally sat down. "Don't you have anything to say?"

I told her she should cool it. She didn't like that. "Joan, Timmy's in the pool, Mother is with him. She wouldn't let anything happen to him." I reasoned.

"It's probably Ronnie's idea to get the pool," she sulked. I laughed. "Hey, I thought you and Doug liked Ronnie?" Joan grumbled.

We stayed a couple of hours more. Joan and I waded in as far as our shorts would allow. Ronnie came home, and he went in with Mother and Timmy.

Soon, we were all laughing and forgetting earlier tensions.

We stayed until seven o'clock. Mother took Timmy in to change, and we said our farewells on the front lawn.

As Joan, Timmy and I got into the car, noise from across the street caught my attention.

"Are those your new neighbors?" I asked, knowing the house had been up for sale. "Do they all live in that house?

"One of them is the woman in the yellow outfit," my Mother replied. "It's a big family. She has five sisters; do you believe it? So, when all get together with husbands and children, it's quite a crowd, like today. One of her sisters just bought a house down the street. Isn't it something how they all look alike?"

CHAPTER 27

I didn't get it. I didn't get it until four o'clock the next morning when I sat up in bed. "They're sisters! Lacey has a sister! She had never mentioned it, but that didn't mean anything. She hadn't said too much about her family except her father had Parkinson's. Lacey was shy, but I expected the more we got to know each other, we probably would have exchanged confidences. That's what I figured anyway, but it didn't happen. After that night we got arrested breaking into The Courier, Lacey had subtly inched away from a friendship with me. Before I knew it, we stopped hanging around together. Each time I asked her to lunch or to do other things, she was always busy. It's funny because I thought she handled that night very well.

Muffy had moved off the bed onto the floor when my revelation came and was staring up at me. "Co'mon Muffy, it's OK. I'm going back to sleep, and you can too. She obediently jumped up and laid her body near me. My mind was churning, but not for long, as sleep overtook both of us.

The next morning, I dropped by Town Hall, but that would have been too easy. A woman told me all records of births and deaths were held in Portland since Sandy Ridge's year-round population was small. It wasn't until April or May that the crowd came to enjoy the ocean and beauty of my town. Then, in October, many older residents went South for the winter. I know I tried to get warmer weather in January or February myself.

The local Town Hall had been a guess anyway since I didn't know if Lacey had been born in Sandy Ridge. It was a beginning.

The local donut shop was hiring. It was right in the center of town, so I planned to go down there today and interview, and then I would go to Portland. My spirits were high as I got dressed; nothing too fancy but clean to present a good image. The local chain, a popular francaise in the area, opened at seven a.m., but I had breakfast, made my bed, cleaned my room a little bit, then put my makeup on and left. It was nine-thirty. Stepping out of my condo, the sun-washed me with its brilliance. It felt warm and toasty. I put my sunglasses on and decided to walk.

The donut shop was busy, but I got a girl's eye and asked to see the manager. She and I interviewed at a small table in the corner of the shop.

The manager was middle-aged and had long, curly, bright, flaming red hair that was a bad dye job, but she smiled a lot and was very chatty. Her name was

Edie, and she kept cracking gum. Edie told me that I would be in the drive-through, wear one of those cute head mikes and take orders that the other girls would fill. If I had time, I would help the other girls with the orders. It paid ten dollars an hour, and if I wanted the job, I could start tomorrow at seven a.m.

"The good part is you get to drink all the coffee you want and eat all the donuts you want," said Edie. She leaned over. "You can even take some home to your kids." She winked at me.

"I don't have any kids," I said. Then I realized she was saying I could pretend they were for my kids, but they were really for me. "I'll take the job," I said. "Do you give me a shirt?"

"Yes. What size are you? We can go in the backroom and get it now."

The bigger question was, what size would I be after I got through having the donuts? "You better give me a large."

Edie brought me back to the storeroom, rummaged through some boxes and came up with a red shirt with the company's logo on it. "You better wash it. The girls, when they leave, are supposed to wash them before they turn them in, but I'm not too sure if you know what I mean."

I took the shirt.

"Now, I'll get you an application form, and you can make that out."

We went into a small room off the storage room, where Edie opened a file drawer and took several pieces of paper out. "You can take these homes and fill them out and bring them in tomorrow if you want."

Edie shook my hand and told me she'd see me the next day. "It's a great bunch of girls here, and the guys are really great. You'll like it."

What could I do but smile back and thank her? Walking home, I decided to call Edie and tell her I didn't want the job. The images of me at two hundred, three hundred pounds still eating donuts were not what I wanted. When I talked to Edie, I'd say something came up, and I'd call her to work when I was free again. But right now, getting to Portland was on my mind. I will get up early tomorrow and call Edie.

Maybe I will call her later today when I get back.

Portland was north of Sandy Ridge, about an hour away. It was lunchtime, and those luscious smells at the donut shop made me hungry. After a combo: cheeseburger, French fries and diet drink, I had the energy to pursue my task, jumped into the car and was off. There was a great talk show on the radio that entertained me as I got on the highway, but thoughts kept coming back concerning the donut shop job. It was a no-brainer, easy, but could I really stay away from the donuts? Edie seemed to be a nice lady, and we got along very well. I could tell she liked me. Humm, maybe it was possible. Needless to say, I wouldn't talk this over with my sponsor. When was the last time I had gone to a diet club meeting? Or eaten correctly?

The drive was highway all the way. The two women on the radio, I would guess, were in their early thirties, completely outrageous, talking about their slant on the news. One was funnier than the other, doing imitations of celebrities making headlines. They had guests on politics, film critics and a meteorologist talking about what to avoid during a lightning storm. Soon, I was driving through the main streets of Portland, my eyes straining to find the Town Hall.

It was in the middle of the square across from a big, sprawling white Congregational Church. I parked in the Town Hall parking lot and walked up the concrete steps. There was a directory in the foyer. Births and deaths were on the second floor. Walking to the elevator, I marveled at the beauty of this Town Hall. There were beautiful, shiny marble floors, and a huge chandelier in the middle of the foyer sparkled because of the sun shining through the many ceiling-to-floor windows over which geraniums hung.

The elevator had marble floors with mirrors on three sides. Elegant was the word that came to mind. It's hard not to check yourself when you have mirrors all around, but I tried to do it without being obvious to the other two people in the elevator. One was a balding businessman with a briefcase, and the other was a young woman about my age carrying two coffees. It must have been an afternoon coffee break. She and I got off together. She went left. I stood there for a minute, getting my bearings.

A heavy, older woman walked by me and asked if she could help me.

"I'm looking for a copy of my birth certificate," I said.

"It's the office on the right around the corner." She left.

Two women were typing, and one was filing when I walked into the office.

They looked at each other, deciding who would help me. The filer won or lost the toss, depending on how you look at it.

"May I help you?" she asked. She was very pretty, in her mid-twenties. Her curly black hair was cropped close to her head. She must have gone to a makeup class or a makeup counter that told her what shades to wear because all of it was just the right coloring for the orange blouse she wore.

I smiled, trying to put my best foot forward, and asked her how she was. "Nice day today," I ventured.

The woman smiled. "Yes, it is. Can I help you?"

"My name is Blaire Nugent, and I'm from Sandy Ridge. I was told that you keep birth certificates for residents of our town."

She nodded.

"Well, I need mine. And, I have a favor to ask of you."

"Yes?" She looked curious now.

"My sister lives out of state, but she would also like a copy of her birth certificate."

"What's her name?"

I paused. She looked at me expectantly.

"Oh my God, I'm having a senior moment, and I'm too young for that." I put my hand up to my forehead, trying to look like I was thinking.

She laughed. And waited.

"Well, she would be another daughter of my mother with the same last name."

"Yeah, but what's her name?"

"Our mother's name is Lacey Miller," I said.

The woman in front of me was getting impatient. "Do you know how many Millers there are in my files? That's a common name."

The woman was not going to budge. Time for the heavy artillery. I took a tissue out of my handbag and started crying. "I don't know her name. I've just found my biological mother. I just found out I have a sister. I want to find her." I was sobbing now. "But my biological mother won't tell me where she is. If I knew her name, I could find her easier."

"So, she isn't out of state like you said."

"Maybe she is. Look, I was desperate, and I needed help. I'm sorry I lied to you, but I must find her."

She looked doubtful and turned to the other two women for support. They shook their heads.

"I'm afraid I can't do that," the orange blouse said.

"Oh, it would mean so much to me," I implored.

The woman looked uncomfortable. One of the typists came over. "We can't do that."

"Why not? I'm told one doesn't need identification to get a copy of their birth certificate, so why should it matter if you check to see if there's another girl born of the same parents?"

"I'm going to have to call my boss," said the typist.

"Please do," I said, putting on a sad face. "This is so important to me."

The typist, whose nameplate said Delores, left and orange blouse went back to filing.

An obese, short guy with a receding hairline and brown mustache came out of his office, not too pleased to be disturbed. I explained my situation, breaking out into tears again. Hmmm, maybe I should try community theater.

"This is highly unethical," he said. "Delores, make Blaire Nugent a copy of her birth certificate. Do you want the card or a copy?"

"Please, you must help me," I tried again.

He shook his head. "I'm sorry. Now, what will it be?"

Cold fish.

"The card." I searched my handbag for a tissue.

He left. Delores came over and handed me the card. "That will be five dollars

Giving her the money, I noticed the other typist giving me a sympathetic look. I put on my best heartbroken face and turned to leave.

"How late are you open?" I asked.

"Till five o'clock." Delores looked puzzled. An idea was hatching in my mind, but I needed time to figure it out.

CHAPTER 28

I was going down the elevator, and my courage was in overdrive. I wasn't going to leave without seeing that birth certificate, so convinced was I that Lacey had a sister.

There was a park down the street. I needed to think this out. The "park" was a maze of beautiful flowers and shrubs called Longfellow's Garden. A plaque said the garden was planted by General Peleg Wadsworth in 1785. He was the grandfather of Henry Wadsworth Longfellow. It was lovely, with fragrant smells and clusters of wooden and ornate benches. First, I dropped in at a cafe down the street and got a coffee to go. On the way back to the park, I noticed a bank and went in and got a couple hundred dollars out of the ATM. Then, back to the park. It was two thirty.

The day had gotten warmer, and it was pleasant sitting in the park drinking my coffee. At three thirty, I decided to walk, but not too far since I wanted to keep an eye on Town Hall.

At quarter of five, I was losing my nerve. Should I get into my car and go back to Sandy Ridge? No, I decided, because I would always wonder about the outcome had I stayed.

At five o'clock, a steady stream of people filed out of Town Hall. I watched from across the street, not wanting anyone to recognize me. Delores, in the orange blouse, came out, chatting and laughing with her coworkers. They were thrilled to be released from their work duties.

I thought I'd missed her, but there she was the sympathetic one. I hurried over. "Hello again," I said.

She wasn't that stupid to believe we just happened to run into each other, and her face showed that.

"Look, can we just talk a minute?"

"Are you stalking me?" she asked, getting nervous.

"No, please hear me out. Let's move over to the curb, and I'll explain myself." She was reluctant but did so.

"I must find my sister. Here I have money, two hundred dollars. All I ask is that you let me into the files and see if I can find my sister's name. The money is yours to keep.

"I noticed you're married. There must be expenses, things you want to buy. You won't be doing anything wrong. Please, I beg you to let me find my sister."

The woman's face took on a horrific look. What was her problem? She only had to let me into her office and let me look through the files. It would take only ten minutes or so.

"Don't be scared. I just want to find my sister," I said.

"What the hell do you think you're doing?" came a booming voice that made me jump. Funny, I wouldn't have thought her fat boss would have a big voice like that.

"If you don't get out of here fast, I'm going to call a cop," he yelled. "It's a Federal offense to try to bribe a state employee."

People were gathering in a circle around us. One thing about me is that I always know when to leave. I shot out of there like a rocket, got in my car, made a U-turn and burned rubber.

The realization of what I had tried to do settled in as I saw the sign saying, "Leaving Portland, Have a Nice Day."

But the trip hadn't been in vain. I had a copy of Blaire's birth certificate and knew in my heart the lady I saw going into the three-decker in Sandy Ridge was Lacey's sister. And I would go on that assumption. Right now, there was a fast food restaurant up ahead, and I was hungry.

An hour later, satiated, I was on the road again, headed toward Sandy Ridge and in a good mood. I was going to take that job at the donut shop. I could handle the temptation and the delicious smells, and if l couldn't, I'd just quit. The caffeine in the diet drinks is great because I was feeling high. That's pretty good, considering I almost got arrested. It was getting to be a habit, almost getting arrested, that was, and I'd have to watch my step from now on.

My watch said a quarter of seven. I was almost at Sandy Ridge and decided to drive over to see if Lacey or her sister were making their daily visit.

Traffic was light, so it didn't take me long to get home. People must have already returned from work and were having supper or watching TV.

Cars were parked on both sides of Prescott Street. I double-parked for a while, hoping someone would come out and leave. Maybe I was too late. I voted to go around the block again, not wanting to miss the strange lady who looked like Lacey. At eight-thirty, there had been no action. I went home.

That night, I made out the donut shop application and washed my shirt. This job could be fun. That's not what I thought, however, when the alarm went off at five in the morning. I pulled my jeans on in a fog, put the shirt on and combed my hair. I grabbed a pair of earrings. I would put them and my lipstick on in the car. Who, in their right mind, gets up at this hour? I wondered.

Edie was her bubbling self, directing her employees. She looked at her watch when I entered.

"Can you get here ten minutes early, Allison? At least until you know the routine."

Earlier? I thought about that. Edie must have thought it didn't require an answer because she walked off, talking to a cluster of girls by the ladies' room.

"Allison, the store is about to open, so today, you'll just make coffee and help the other girls when they need it. You can introduce yourself and, as time permits, get to know each other. Come with me."

I followed Edie. "It gets very busy when we first open because of all the people going to work," she explained.

"Joanne, show Allison how to make the coffee."

Edie left. Joanne introduced herself. "The first day is always confusing.

"Don't pay any mind to Edie. She gets this way sometimes.

"I'll call out my coffee order, and you just have to put the cream or sugar into the coffee before you fill the cup," said Joanne. She showed me where the small, medium, large and extra-large cups were, and the cream and the sugar.

"Extra sugar is two teaspoons, and coffee light is two helpings," Joanne instructed.

"What is a helping?" I asked.

Joanne put some cream into a cup to show me. "We share the tips.

There's a cup in front of the register, and at the end of the day, we split it." She shrugged. "It isn't very much. Somehow, people don't think to tip the girl that's pouring their coffee or getting them donuts."

I gave her a sympathetic look.

"The coffee's already been made," continued Joanne, "but when it's half down, you must prepare another batch to go into the coffee pot and pour the last of the old coffee into a paper cup."

Joanne looked out the window. "Geez, look at the line outside. She glanced at her watch. "Two minutes to go. Do you think you'll be alright?"

I nodded, thinking this was not unlike a marathon.

Edie went to the door and glanced back at everybody. "You ready?" We nodded. What else could we do?

"OK, boys, take your time," Edie said to the blue suiters rushing in. "There's plenty to go around."

I couldn't distinguish Joanne's voice from the other girls, but I kept pouring.

"No, I wanted mine without sugar," someone said. Joanne looked at me as if I had sinned. "The lady wants no sugar," she whispered. I nodded and gave her several doses of cream. Oh, Lord, I hope she wanted it light.

By mid-morning, it began to slow down. Good thing. My arm was beginning to hurt. Edie came over. "You're giving them too much cream," she said. "Lift the nozzle once, but don't hold it," she said and showed me. "Just a quick motion up and down. That's all."

Edie walked away from me. She must have made a face because the girl in front of her smirked and looked back at me. Oh, great. I can't even pour a cup of coffee correctly. I was exhausted, and it was only noontime.

Joanne came over. "It was really wild here this morning with all these people, but you did alright. Don't worry about Edie. She doesn't stay mad."

I hadn't realized she was mad.

"How's the coffee?" asked Joanne. "Do you need to make another pot of regular and decaf?"

I started to dump the coffee in the sink. Joanne yelled to put it in a cup. "Remember I told you that? And make sure you clean it out good."

I did as I was told. The rest of the day went slowly. I pondered giving my notice. I was tired.

The next day, I was dragging at the donut shop. Edie fussed because I didn't get in early again. I promised I would the next day. Apparently, every day was a nightmare between the hours of seven and nine a.m. Because today, the mob was out the door. Personally, I didn't think their coffee was that good. The donuts did look yummy because I was trying not to look at them.

Joanne and I were becoming fast friends, but today, she was short with me and snotty. She kept asking me to go faster. Man, my eyes were so tired. I wanted to sprawl out on the floor and take a nap. At break time, Joanne apologized, and I did, too.

"It's that time of the month," my friend said.

I nodded. Sorry, I'm not swift today. I had a late night, and it's hard getting up these early hours.:

"Why don't you make up some with sugar already in them, and that way you could just put the cream in and fill it with coffee," Joanne offered.

"I can't seem to get the hang of the sugar. It comes out too quickly, and one time, Edie saw me, and she reminded me that sugar prices are high. I guess someone complained about too much sugar in their coffee, and she had to give them another coffee."

Joanne looked like that was an incredulous statement to her, and walked away.

At lunchtime, I plied myself with caffeine soft drinks, thinking that would keep me awake, but the afternoon dragged on. Ted came bouncing through the door. This must be his regular stop every day. Terrific!

"Geez, Allison, you don't look so good."

"Thanks, Ted, I really needed that."

"What happened? Did you have a late date last night?"

"As a matter of fact, I did."

"Tell him to get you home earlier. You need your beauty sleep," Ted laughed.

"What makes you think I went home, Ted."

That shut him up. He ordered the same as yesterday. Coffee and a coconut cream donut.

"Be careful, Ted, you're going to gain weight if you keep on eating those."

"Looks like you already have," he said, giving me the exact change and exiting.

He looked back at me and chuckled. I wanted to go after him and crush the donut right in his face.

Joanne was observing the discourse between Ted and me, and she came over.

"He's a rat," she said.

I smiled through the tears in my eyes.

She handed me a Kleenex. "Why don't you go home? I can tell Edie you weren't feeling well."

"That'll go over well, the second day on the job. No, just give me a few minutes, and I'll regain my composure, such as it is. Besides, you're the one with the cramps. Are you leaving early?"

"I'll see how the afternoon goes. If it's not that busy, maybe I will."

Talking to Joanne made me feel better, but I went into the restroom, splashed water on my face and put some lipstick on. The rest of the day was uneventful. Students came in after school between two and three p.m. every day, and the place got loud. Then, around four p.m., until I got off work, harried workers straggled in for a cup of coffee and a donut to help them on the commute home.

The clock had been crawling since noon, but finally, five p.m. came, and I went home. Muffy greeted me and wrapped herself around my leg. I stumbled to the couch to take a nap.

Have you ever been so tired you can't sleep? You start to nap. Then, when your head goes down, you wake up with a start. That's what happened to me. Finally, I got up. Muffy wanted to go out. I let her out through the sun deck and then started to make supper. I boiled two eggs and put them on some greens. Yummy. After dinner, I just couldn't settle down. I tried TV for a while, but that didn't interest me. I wrote out some bills. Muffy came in. I fed her.

The clock said I'd better retire for the night if I wanted to get in ten minutes earlier at the donut shop and make Edie happy. Instead, I grabbed my purse and headed for the door. Once outside in my car, it turned automatically toward Prescott Street. It was around ten p.m. The habit of doing something instinctively was going to get me into trouble someday. I hoped it wasn't tonight.

In front of the apartment house, I called the fire department, reporting a fire at eight, nine and ten Prescott Street.

Three engines came, their sirens howling down the street. I felt guilty as hell, but in defense of myself, I didn't know what else to do. The firefighters rushed into the building with hoses set. I heard them yell:" fire, fire." People came out in swarms, fear in their eyes evident. My conscience was working overtime. I got out of the car and ran over close to the apartment building. People were hugging each other in sadness and grief. Oh, I'll have to go to confession for this.

Lacey must have gone home because I didn't see her. I searched the crowd, looking for her sister, and finally saw her in the crowd. Why had I done this? Adults were crying. Children were screaming. It was crazy of me to do this. Was I losing my perspective as Ted told me? Maybe I needed psychiatric care?

Then I saw Susan, the girl I had known as Blaire. She was standing against the covering of a tree, but I knew it was her. She had gotten separated from her aunt. Probably, her aunt had told her to stay in the dark where nobody could see her.

It took 30 minutes for the firefighters to check every apartment. They didn't look too happy when they came out and yelled, "False alarm."

Relieved, everybody started marching back into the building. Lacey's sister was talking to someone. I moved toward where Susan was standing. She didn't even notice me. She was probably waiting for her aunt to come and get her.

"Well, Blaire, or is it Susan? We meet again."

Chapter 29

Susan was shocked and bewildered at seeing me. "How come you're surprised to see me?" I asked. "We are roommates, after all."

The girl didn't hear the sarcasm in my voice. She was speechless and appeared ill-equipped to deal with me. I needed to take advantage of that.

"Susan, we have to talk."

Blaire, or Susan, whoever she was calling herself these days, looked terrified. Funny, I never thought I could have that effect on anybody. I tried a different approach. Putting my hand on her arm, I told her how worried I was when she disappeared after going out to cover a meeting for The Courier.

"You have no idea how scared I was that something happened to you. But tell me, have you been staying here all this time? And, if you have, what happened to you that night? Why didn't you feel that you could call me and tell me where you were?"

I heard the crunching of leaves behind me and turned. Lacey's sister was giving me the evil eye.

"Susan, we have to go into the house now. It's getting cold out here, and it's late."

I turned to Susan. "A lot of people have been looking for you. Come with me now, and we'll tell them you're alive and well."

Her aunt stepped forward. "Susan's not going anywhere with you."

"Who is Susan to you?" I asked. Turning to the girl, I asked her if this woman was her aunt. The girl crumbled in front of me, crying softly at first and then more loudly.

"Susan has been under a great deal of strain," Lacey's sister said, stepping forward and taking the girl by the arm. "Now, if you'll excuse us."

"So, has everybody else that has been looking for her," I said. I knew in the worst scenario, I could overtake the woman, but I wasn't sure about the two of them. Should Susan try to protect this woman whom I knew to be her aunt? I really didn't know what Susan would do. She wasn't acting as I had known her, and the aunt was being very protective of her.

"An idea just occurred to me," I said. Turning to Susan but including the other, I said, "Why don't we all go in my car to see Police Chief Hall, and then, you can take Susan home after that. Then, Susan, your disappearance is explained, and everybody's happy."

Was anybody buying this? I knew I wasn't.

"Susan isn't well enough to go anywhere," Jess protested.

"Why, what's wrong with her?" I looked at Susan. Her hair was unkempt; looking closely, I even saw knots in her hair, like it hadn't been combed in a long time. She wasn't the confident girl that had been my roommate. Susan's posture was bad, her shoulders slumped, her eyes vacant. Was she using drugs? Where did she get them?

"What is wrong with Susan?" I asked. Her protector said it was hard to explain.

"Let's go to the police station, then we can get her a doctor. Susan is acting strange. For instance, why isn't she talking?"

To my question, Lacey's sister stepped forward, grabbed Susan and started toward the house. The girl acted like a mop that had just been rinsed out. I didn't understand that, but I couldn't let her go.

I grabbed the woman and pushed her against a tree. "Don't hurt me," she cried. "Don't hurt me."

"I'm not going to hurt you. Why don't you go down to police headquarters with me and Susan? Then you can bring her back. It's OK. Nobody needs to get hurt." Might as well take advantage of the situation. If she thought I was tough, that could count in my favor.

"Let me first introduce myself," I said. My name is

Allison Peters and I work with Lacey and Susan was my roommate for a time. But I don't know your name." I smiled, hoping to maybe get into the woman's good graces. At this point, it didn't seem possible, but miracles do happen.

Chapter 30

The woman was guarded but told me her name was Jess and she was Lacey's sister.

"I know. You look so much alike. I extended my hand. After a moment she took it and we shook hands.

"Let's go up into the apartment. Susan is cold," she said.

I followed the women up. They offered me tea and I said yes. We sat there looking at each other. Finally, I reiterated what I had said before, how we needed to help Susan. "People have been searching for her for weeks and it would be good to see what is exactly wrong with Susan. Let's give Susan a better life than she's having now," I begged Jess.

It took time, but Jess agreed. "I have to call Lacey first."

I agreed. Jess called her. I got on the line to persuade her. Or, I thought I had. But Lacey wanted to talk further with me about what might happen to Susan and to Jess and her for harboring Susan.

I told them that Police Chief Ed Hall was compassionate and he would understand. Jess and

Susan weren't going anywhere without Lacey though, but I finally convinced my friend and Lacey said she would come over and we would all go to the police station together. I figured she was stalling for time, that maybe Lacey thought she could talk me out of going to the police station. I would give her this time, but in the end, we were going to turn Susan into Hall.

I still thought of Lacey as my friend, but I knew that maybe, in the end, she wouldn't be. Lacey took her time getting to Jess's apartment, and it looked like maybe she wasn't coming, but three-quarters of an hour later, there was the sound of a key in the lock, and it was Susan's mother.

Now, all three of them looked at me. At this point, I told Lacey to sit down. She did.

"What doesn't make sense to me is, why hide Susan? In this day, there are plenty of single mothers. No one would say anything if Susan became a part of your life."

"Our father mustn't know she's here," said Jess. "If he saw her, our father would tell her to go away."

"In his illness, your father might like to have a grandchild around, even a grown one," I countered.

"Not the way Susan's been acting," said Jess, shaking her head.

Bingo!!! "Yeah, what is wrong with Susan anyway? You said she was having terrible nightmares."

"We had to quiet her down, so we gave her our father's tranquilizers," explained Jess.

"You damn fool!" Lacey shouted at Jess. It took a minute for Jess to understand that, in her naivete, she had brought the conversation to where I had wanted it.

It was amazing how everything had just unfolded so easily. Jess hadn't realized she admitted to something that was a secret. In our comradery over the tea and Danish, we were three women chatting and bearing our souls. I had a feeling Jess really wanted to get out from under whatever she was helping Lacey cover up anyway.

"Lacey, what is the big deal here anyway?" I asked. "Being her mother, I should think you'd want to help Susan put her past behind her so she could get on with her life. Susan is a young woman, and it's best for her to settle whatever is bothering her now.

Did I sound convincing? Had I heard that piece of advice on Oprah? It had that Oprah sound if you know what I mean?

I was on a roll. "Susan is not happy. You keep her locked up as if she's a prisoner. It's not the way for you and Jess to live."

Lacey's teary eyes looked into mine. I dared not blink.

"Do you know the heavy burden that I've had since Susan found me?"

"Let it go, then," I whispered.

"When Susan told me she was your roommate, I was thrilled. In my heart, I felt you would be a good influence on her," Lacey said.

"But I never had a chance. Susan disappeared. What was that all about? Where did she go, and with whom? And why did she call herself Blaire Nugent? Why not use her own name? Who is Blaire Nugent?"

Lacey smiled, her face imploring me to understand. "Susan thought that finding me would give her a new beginning. She didn't want to use a name that had brought her so much heartache."

"Lacey." I took my friend's hand in compassion, but also, I didn't want her to go anywhere.

"Who is Blaire Nugent?"

She didn't speak. Out there in the electric air space, I heard Jess say, "Blaire Nugent was Lacey's other daughter and Susan's half-sister. But then I think you knew that, didn't you?"

I nodded.

"So, Blaire and Susan were sisters? Were they twins?"

"No," said Jess. "I told you they were sisters."

"Oh, so you did. What happened to Blaire?" I asked Jess. "Did you or Lacey kill her?"

Before Jess could answer, Lacey piped up, "How could I kill my own child?"

"Then what or who are you hiding Susan from? Did Susan kill her sister because she wanted you all to herself?"

"Susan loved her sister, Blaire," said Lacey.

"Someone didn't," I said. "Blaire suffered a terrible death. That person viciously took Blaire's head and banged it against a rock. Police Chief Hall says Blaire died after the third blow, but the killer kept banging her head ten more times. If you care anything about your oldest child, Blaire, then you must help us find whoever did it. So, I'm going to ask you again: did Susan kill Blaire?"

My tone was steady, and my face never left Lacey's. The woman looked trapped. Her face became ashen, her eyes were already bloodshot, and her posture bent and frail as an old woman.

"Tell her, my sister. Tell her," advised Jess gently.

The silence was louder than any high school football rally. When she spoke, it was deliberate and slow, as a person in speech therapy.

"Blaire followed Susan to Sandy Ridge. She thought Susan was going to do something crazy and ruin everyone's life. Blaire thought I was married and had other children, and Susan would not be greeted favorably by me. Blaire, I heard, had been brought up by a wonderful family and was very secure at least until Susan came into her life.

"Susan told me she didn't know Blaire had followed her to Sandy Ridge, and then when Susan saw her in the parking lot the night she went to cover that meeting of the Rod and Gun Club, Susan was frantic. Susan kept asking Blaire to come away with her, but my youngest daughter was adamant; she had found me and was going to find her father.

"The two girls got into an argument in the parking lot. Susan was afraid someone from the meeting was going to hear, so they moved into the woods that surrounded the clubhouse. Susan was tougher than Blaire. She's had to fight for everything most of her life. Apparently, from what Susan said, she and Blaire were yelling at each other. Susan told Blaire to go home. Blaire grabbed Susan and tried to pull her away. She wanted Susan to come back to her car and talk.

"Susan has a temper. She pushed Blaire, hoping the girl would get scared and leave. Blaire lost her footing and, in trying to catch herself, fell against a tree. Susan told me her sister was winded but not seriously hurt."

"Did Blaire get up again?"

"Yes, and she started yelling at Susan again. Susan pushed her up against a tree and socked her. That's when she left. Susan told me she drove around for hours, not sure of what to do. She realized she had hit Blaire too hard. At about two in the morning, Susan went back to find Blaire. That's when she found her dead. As you can imagine, Susan was out of her mind with grief, at what she had done. That's when she came to me. I couldn't keep her at my place, so I called Jess. You know the rest of the story."

Would Lacey take Susan in after admitting she killed her sister? It didn't make sense, I thought. What kind of a mother would do that?

Looking at Lacey, I somehow believed her, even knowing I wouldn't have reacted that way. She probably figured after all this time, one child was better than nothing.

"Weren't you afraid that Susan would hurt you and Jess?"

"She was acting so strange. I guess maybe we were," admitted Jess. She looked remorseful. "We started giving her the pills right away. They're only an antidepressant. We thought it would help Susan calm down until we figured out what to do."

Lacey told me they didn't mean any harm, and she and Jess did whatever they had to do. Her tone was defensive and almost belligerent.

What is the cliché, the blind leading the blind? I thought. I got up.

"Where are you going?" Lacey asked, panicky.

"You must tell your story to Police Chief Hall." I moved back to the table. "It's the only way."

"What will he do with Susan?"

I told her I didn't know. My friend was beginning to bug me. I told her she had a responsibility to her other child, Blaire, and that she must know that in her heart.

"Will Hall keep all that I tell him confidential? I just wouldn't want this on the front page of The Courier. For my father's sake."

"Hall is a great guy. For the length of time I've known him, he's been professional, compassionate and understanding. He certainly puts up with me."

Lacey nodded. She was worried but agreed to tell her story to Hall. Tiredness was seeping through my whole body. My heart and my bones ached; my heart for Lacey and her family; my bones because I looked at my watch, and it was six in the morning. I knew I wouldn't be dishing out donuts and coffee at Edie's today.

It took more convincing, but in the end, Lacey knew Jess was in favor of going to see Police Chief Hall.

"Let's put an end to all of this lying and sneaking around and let it be done," said Jess.

I was really impressed with her common sense, a trait I thought none of these women possessed.

We went in two cars. Lacey, Jess and Susan in one and I drove myself. The police station was a couple of streets over, and we were there in no time. I honestly thought there was a chance Lacey might take off, and I would be left, but maybe something I said made sense to her because they were the first to arrive and were waiting for me.

We in together. The dispatcher announced us, and Hall told us to come in.

When we went in, Hall looked up. He had met Lacey but did not know Jess and Susan, so he looked to me for introductions, which I did. He motioned for all of us to gather around a circular table with chairs for all of us. He then looked at me to take the lead.

"Lacey, Jess and Susan have something to tell you," I said. He moved past me and sat down next to the woman.

"You'll forgive me if I go home now," I told the group. The sisters put up their hands to protest, but I stood my ground.

"Lacey, I'll do everything I can to help you. Chief, I'll talk to you later."

"I'm not talking to anybody without you here, Allison."

Ah sh....!

"I can't tell how it happened again," said Lacey. "It's too painful."

I sat down.

Hall looked at me to explain. "Lacey, tell the Chief what happened the night Blaire Nugent was killed. You told me you can tell it again. I'm here for you," I said.

Lacey started slow and weak but got louder and clearer with time. She told Hall that what she was about to reveal must be kept confidential. He agreed.

The woman began repeating what she had told me. Isn't it strange how some single mothers want so desperately to find their biological children they put up for adoption? Lacey had prayed for that day when she would see her two children and, as the fairy tale says, live happily ever after with them in her life. I doubted Lacey would live a day without guilt and remorse that maybe if she had done something, anything, the outcome would have been different. Lacey looked twice her age. Jess was staring into space, wondering how she got into this mess, and I vowed to sleep for days when this night, or morning, was over.

Hall had taken out his notebook and was listening to what Lacey said. Even Lacey looked a little bored. Maybe I should have had Hall in the room the first time, but I was afraid Lacey wouldn't be as candid.

I tried to remember if anyone had died from lack of sleep. It took about twenty minutes for Lacey to tell what Susan had told her about that night.

Hall asked several questions. Jess chimed in with what Lacey had left out. I got a twitch in my leg.

When Hall was satisfied, he told Lacey that he would lock Susan up for the night and advised her to get a lawyer for her daughter.

"There are several good ones in town. I'll write their names for you before you leave." I looked over at Susan. She was dozing. Had Lacey given her a sleeping pill?

Hall asked if there was something wrong with Susan. Lacey explained she was giving her daughter pills that her father was taking just to calm her down.

"You know you can't do that," said Hall. "I think it would be a good idea if you were with me when we wake her up in a few minutes. You can also explain to her what has and will happen."

"What do you mean?" asked Lacey.

"I mean the fact that Susan will have to stay in jail until her arraignment."

"When will that be?"

In so many instances, I have found Hall to be compassionate, but I think in this one, he was definitely being challenged. The Police Chief didn't answer Lacey but got up and started walking toward his office. We all followed Lacey beside Hall. He explained to her what was going to happen and reiterated her need to get a lawyer. Hall went to his desk, opened the front drawer, drew out several business cards and gave them to Lacey.

"Say that I recommended them." Hall went back to where Susan was sleeping. I heard Susan wake up and Lacey explain what was going to happen. She would stay in jail; her mother would get Susan a lawyer. The young woman didn't take it too well and was screaming obscenities and dragging her feet. With the help of officers, Susan was dragged into the jail cell.

In all the excitement, with everyone looking at Susan, Ted had come in the door to work. I looked at his donut and realized I hadn't called in sick at Edie's. Yikes!

I asked Ted if I could use his cell phone, dialed Edie's, put a finger on my nose to sound nasal and told her I wouldn't be in. Edie was solicitous and told me to feel better. That surprised me, but I was grateful. I turned my attention again to the situation at hand. Dare, I hope to go home soon.

Jess wanted to visit with Susan in her cell. Hall thought better of that and told her to stay in his office. He would need her last name, address and telephone number, as well as a statement from her. The same went for Lacey.

"Geez, Allison, you look like you've been up all night," said Ted, wisecracking. He had been studying what was going on around him but still wasn't too sure what was happening and wanted me to elaborate. By now, Ted was devouring his donut and slurping his coffee at his desk.

What a slob, I thought.

I was then distracted by the noise coming from the cell. Apparently, Lacey had gone into the cell, trying to soothe her daughter.

"You betrayed me, you traitor," the girl yelled at Lacey. "This is all your fault. You betrayed me. You're a lousy mother, anyway. I don't need you."

When Lacey came within view of Ted and me, her face was in complete devastation. With a daughter like Susan, Lacey had to develop a tougher shell.

Susan was yelling all the way down the corridor to the cells. I heard the cell door rattle. I still heard her when Hall shut the outer door leading into the cells, and I went over to comfort Lacey.

Ted idled over to me and asked what had happened during the night.

"Ask Hall." Glancing over at the Chief, I asked if we could all leave.

"Lacey and Jess have to give me their statements. You can leave." That was music to my ears until Lacey asked me to stay. I sat down.

Ted came over. "It looks like I've been up all night because I have, so don't be such an asshole," I said. To which he returned to his desk. I closed my eyes, but the chairs at police headquarters weren't conducive to sleep.

The time seemed endless, but Lacey and Jess eventually came out, and we left.

"Jess, why don't you drive," I suggested. "Lacey, get some sleep, and when you wake up, call one of those lawyers. Susan's just upset right now. She'll get over it. You and Jess are the only people she's got. When Susan calms down, she'll realize that."

I gave both women a hug, waited until they drove off and went over to my car.

The day felt crisp and had a clean smell to it. The darkness of the night had given way to the light of morning. The cool air felt good, and I put my windows down driving off. With my luck, the caffeine from the coffee would keep me from sleeping. But that wasn't the case. In fact, I don't remember my head hitting the pillow.

At eight o'clock that evening, I woke up. At first, I didn't know where I was, but then I got my bearings. I went to the kitchen, fixed myself a sandwich, drank some water and returned to bed. I woke up at seven the next morning, took a long, hot shower, dressed and made my way to the Police Station. It was then I realized I hadn't called Edie's. I used my cell phone, still putting a finger over one nostril in an effort to sound nasally and congested.

Edie told me she missed seeing my pretty face, which meant either she was gay and hot for my body or she knew I was faking and I needed to get to work the following day. I surmised the latter to be true but made a mental note to keep an eye on Edie.

Hall looked tired but managed a smile when he saw me.

"Well, hot shot detective, have you come to get our cold case files to investigate further wrongdoings in Sandy Ridge?"

"No, I came to see Susan. How is she doing?"

Hall indicated I should take a seat and told me the girl had stopped cursing Lacey and now was complaining about the food.

"Lacey came in early this morning to bring Susan some personal items she'll need."

"That's good," I said. "Chief, what do you think about Susan's story?"

Hall grimaced. "I think she killed Blaire. Maybe Susan lost her temper. We've seen that she has one. She had a knife on her."

I hadn't known that.

"This is just speculation. Susan told Lacey she had a fight with Blaire and socked her. Blaire could have gotten up and persisted. By then, Susan was in a fury, took out a knife and stabbed her numerous times."

"Do you really believe that's what happened?"

"Allison, we have no other suspects. Susan told Lacey she was there; she had an argument with Blaire. They fought. You even told me Susan came from a tough life; it could be, once she gets in a fight, she doesn't remember what she does."

"When is she being arraigned?"

"Lacey was going to see Merlin Brown after visiting Susan. He's a good lawyer," said Hall.

"It was good of you to give her his name."

Hall told me he felt sorry for Lacey. "She seemed so frightened and confused when she was in here. I'm glad Lacey has Jess, but neither one has encountered something like this before."

"Can I see Susan now?"

"Ten minutes. No more." Hall gave me one of his fatherly but stern looks. I was the wayward daughter.

Susan didn't even look up when I approached. "What do you want?"

"I'm here to help you if you'll let me." She snorted. "Some help you've been."

"I don't believe you did it."

She looked up for the first time. "Who are you, girl private detective? Nobody has ever helped me, and you don't look like you could make your way out of a paper bag."

I didn't want to get into it with Susan. "Looks are deceiving. Let me help," I said.

Not waiting for another thought about me from Susan, I asked, "Were you and Blaire alone when you were fighting in the woods?"

She did a double take. "What do you think we invited people to watch?"

"Concentrate Susan. Were there people milling around from the Rod and Gun Club meeting, someone who could have seen you two? You were out in the parking lot. Was the meeting over?"

The girl didn't say anything for what appeared to be a long time but instead was studying me.

"Well?" I encouraged.

"The bed in here stinks, ya know. Can you get me an upgrade?"

"If you help me figure this out, you'll be out of here," I said.

Susan mulled that over. "How do I know I can trust you?" she asked. "You're the one who got me in here."

"No, Susan, I'm not the one, and I believe you know that deep down. But I can help you if you'll let me. What do you say?"

She shrugged. "I have nothing to lose. I came out late the night of the Rod and Gun Club meeting. They were only winding up anyway. I saw who I wanted to see in the meeting, and I was waiting for the crowd to leave. I didn't want him to get away."

"Was it your father? Is that why you wanted that assignment?" I asked.

"Yeah."

This confused me because I knew Shaw hadn't gone to that meeting.

"If you blackmailed Shaw for the assignment, how come you were waiting for him after the meeting?" I asked.

"What are you talking about?" Susan wanted to know. She realized what I had said and started laughing. In fact, she really howled and thought that was the funniest thing she had ever heard.

I felt myself blushing. "Shaw's not your father? Then how did you get to cover the Rod and Gun Club meeting with no experience?" Susan was pointing her finger at me and laughing uproariously.

"This isn't funny, Susan. If you think it is, then I'll leave," and I started walking toward the Chief's office.

Susan sobered up fast. "No, no, I do need your help. Please come back."

"How come you got the assignment?"

"I told him I was Lacey's daughter and I was looking for my father. But I needed a job. His face dropped down to his shoes. I guess he and Lacey warmed the sheets at one time, and he felt guilty. I let him think whatever he wanted."

"So, you know it wasn't Shaw, but someone else?"

Susan started to say something, but I couldn't hear her because of Hall's booming voice.

"Times up," he yelled. Scared the you-know-what out of me.

Susan looked amused. I asked her whom she wanted to confront after the meeting that night.

"You'd love to know, wouldn't you?" she retorted. "No, this is my ace in the hole. If you think I'm going to let anyone else approach him, you're crazy. I want to see the look on his face when I tell him who I am."

"Suppose he doesn't care; suppose he brushes you off."

Susan looked dead on at me. "We'll see how his family likes the news, how his wife and children react. This is a small town, Allison. Stories have a habit of growing like wildfire."

Hall opened the door again. "Don't you hear well?"

"Just a sec, Chief."

"No, now."

I asked Susan if there was anything she needed.

"Yeah, get me out of here."

There was nothing I could say to that, so I left.

CHAPTER 31

Out in my car, I mused about Susan being so sure of herself. Her biological father had been at the Rod and Gun Club that night; she had planned to confront him, but her fight with Blaire interfered.

I thought about the sea of faces interested in the Rod and Gun Club getting the permanent liquor license for the club. It also could be the opposition. Susan only knew she needed to confront this guy; she wanted to disgrace him, humiliate him, and get even with him for years lost because he abandoned her and Lacey.

Who could this guy be?

I went across the street to a rival coffee shop. Just my luck, Edie would be passing by and see me. Thinking about that, I chose a corner table in the back. The waitress took my order of coffee and English Muffins. The day's newspaper was on an adjoining table. I snatched it up, realizing I hadn't been keeping up with town news lately.

The Courier was a good newspaper, and residents inhaled it. It's good public relations to have one on hand at restaurants and coffee shops. Edie's Coffee

Shop does it, and it's a nice convenience for those who don't get a newspaper delivered to their door.

My heart did a flip-flop when I noticed on page 56 that The Courier was looking for staff reporters. Applicants should apply to Bill Shaw, Suburban Editor, at the newspaper.

How long had the ad been in the newspaper, and was the position already filled? Did I dare to apply? The job certainly came at a perfect time, since I realized I needed to apologize to Shaw because of my behavior over the last couple of months. I had thought he was Susan's father. Well, he thought so too, I guess, because he gave Susan the reporter job when she told him she was Lacey's daughter. True, Susan had let him assume a lot of things, but Shaw had taken the bait.

The English Muffins melted in my mouth. I hadn't had them in years, and the melted butter on them was heavenly. In fact, I was so enthralled with what I was eating I almost missed it.

On page 76, under local news, Burt Olsen was at it again. It said that the Road and Gun Club asked to be put on the Selectmen's agenda to talk about getting their permanent liquor license. I knew the Selectmen had given the club a temporary six-month license, and I hadn't heard they had any infractions at all, but, of course, I was out of the loop now anyway having been fired. Had it been six months already? I didn't think so. Why then would Selectmen want to hear from them at all?

The article quoted Olson's usual tirade against the license, but this time, the club was desperate because Colin Reed was having second thoughts about donating the land. I had heard that a while ago. Apparently, he hadn't changed his mind.

On a hunch, I called Olsen on my cell phone. "Where have you been?" he asked.

I explained that I no longer worked for The Courier, but I saw the article in the newspaper and wanted to know why Colin Reed was withdrawing his land offer.

"I've still got a reporter's curiosity," I said.

"Reed's a politician. The liquor license issue is taking too long, I guess, and he's never been one to mess with the Selectmen, who wish this controversy would go away."

"You should know by now that the town fathers don't want to tax their brains with difficult decisions," I said.

Olson agreed.

"We'll just have to see what happens," said Olsen. "Without his land, the club is a small strip, and Sam Davis' dreams of enlarging the club won't happen, and you know that would be OK by me."

I rang off with Olson. A reporter's draw for a good story was making me unsettled, but I was torn whether to get into that again, provided Shaw hired me back. I knew I must apologize to Shaw for my behavior, which got me fired. I would do that regardless of whether he would hire me back. As far as I knew, Shaw still thought Susan was his daughter. I didn't know whether it was up to me to tell him any different.

I motioned to the waitress for another cup of coffee and called Lacey. She had called that morning. We talked briefly. Her nerves were raw. She told me, and she was afraid. I again told her I would help her in any way that I could.

Lacey's father said she was over Jess's apartment. "Could I have that coffee to go? " I asked the waitress. It took only a minute. I should have gone home, in case Edie tried to call me, but instead decided to go over to Jess' apartment instead. I wanted to find out from Lacey what lawyer she had hired and what they think would be Susan's defense.

Driving over to Jess' place, my conversation with Olson came back to me. I missed working at The Courier. I had to admit that.

On Jess' street, I easily pulled into a space opposite the apartment. Draining the last of the coffee, I threw the cup into my car's little bag with the prowess of a basketball star. I was suddenly in a good mood and realized I liked not working and having the day off to myself.

I crossed the street deep in thought about how I could support myself and not work at Edie's.

Crossing the wide expanse of lawn, it's a miracle they didn't see me. But I was lost in my own thoughts, walking boldly toward the building. The couple were arguing loudly at each other. Then I noticed the woman was Lacey. She was flying her arms wildly, and he was gritting his teeth at her. I ran for cover at a nearby tree, all too aware it did not cover me completely. If the couple turned to the right, I would be exposed. I willed myself be invisible.

What I saw put everything into perspective. The jigsaw puzzle fell into place. Why couldn't the tree be as broad as me? Thankfully, the couple in front of me were so engrossed in their argument they were oblivious to anything else. Now Lacey was pounding on the man's chest, crying, and he looked like he was going to belt her. Uh-oh. He picked her up by the shoulders and put her a safe distance away from him.

"You're crazy," he shouted, leaving.

Geez, what are the neighbors thinking? Thinking about it, I knew no one cared.

Lacey continued crying while the man got into his car and left. I held my breath lest he see me behind the tree as he drove up off.

Luck was with me. Lacey returned to the house. I looked at my watch and stayed behind for three minutes. Yes, I did time it and then ran to my car.

What was I going to do with what I had just seen? I had thought I would leave once back in the car but decided instead to pay Lacey a visit. That had been my original idea, to visit her and comfort her. And I still wanted to know what lawyer Lacey chose.

Lacey's eyes were red when she opened the door of Jess' apartment, and she was not happy to see me.

"Have I come at a bad time?"

"No, it's just that I've made bail for Susan, and I'm going now to drive her home."

"That's great news. I didn't know bail had been set."

"The arraignment was this morning. Susan's lawyer is Marianne Cole, and she seems quite good. Heaven knows we need a miracle." Blaire said she had decided a woman would be best for Susan.

"How much is the bail?" I asked.

Twenty-five thousand dollars."

"Yipes. Where did you come up with that?"

"Allison, I can't talk now. I want to get Susan, "Lacey was moving toward the door and hoping I'd do the same.

"Oh, sure, I understand. Why don't I call you later?"

Lacey rushed ahead of me. She wanted to get her kid out of jail as soon as possible. I understood that. Had she gotten the $25,000 from the biological father? I knew the father to be financially successful, but how was he going to explain to his wife that much money was missing from their account?

I pondered my options in light of Lacey's news, picked up my cell phone and called Hall.

"I just talked to Lacy. She's on the way over to get Susan. Did you tell the judge you're afraid of her taking off?"

"Allison, let the police handle this. As much as you think you're hot on the trail, the police know what they're doing. Besides, Lacey made bail. My hands are tied. Now, if you'll let me get back to work. . . "

Hall hung up on me. I didn't believe it. I was right not to tell Hall about the guy Lacey was talking to in front of Jess' apartment. I would crack this case myself, and he'd be sorry for his attitude.

I pulled out of the parking space and made tracks for the police station, staying a half block away in case Lacey or Susan recognized my car. To tell you the truth, I didn't know what my next move would be.

Susan and Lacey came out of the station a half hour later. I got out and went up to them. Lacey's look indicated disbelief. I talked fast.

"Susan, your mother told me you were making bail today. I just wanted to wish you good luck."

Susan gave me a dirty look. Can you imagine?

"We really have to go," said Lacey. The woman started toward her car, Susan following behind.

"If you need anything, just call," I said.

They didn't say a word but got in the car. I waited until they passed and waved. They stared straight ahead. When the car got out of view, I rushed into police headquarters.

"Well, well, well, I kind of figured I'd see you today," said Hall.

"Are you going to put a tail on Susan?" I asked, ignoring Hall's sarcasm. Ted came in from the outer office.

"Doesn't anyone else work here?"

Hall came over to me. He was not happy.

"Allison, let me tell you again. Apparently, you're hard of hearing. This is police business, and you may not think so, but we know what we're doing."

"She knows who her biological father is, and Susan is going to look him up."

"No kidding. You're brilliant," said Hall. Turning to Ted, he said, "We should sign her up for police training. Then she could become one of us."

"God forbid," was Ted's answer.

I gave them both a dirty look and left. This case was getting to Hall. He had never acted so touchy before. Well, I would show Hall . . . and Ted.

I didn't think Susan would make any moves toward her biological father tonight in case Hall was tailing her. I went by Jess's apartment to make sure Lacey's car was there. It was. There was nothing to do but go home, which I did.

The next morning, I was back in front of Jess' early. Lacey's car had not moved during the night. I parked down the street with an easy view of their building, munching on my sausage and egg muffin and drinking my beverage. I had gotten two cups of coffee but was reluctant to drink the second in case I had to pee.

At two in the afternoon, after no action from the apartment, I went to lunch. When I returned to Lacey's, the car was in the same spot. They must be lying low. I stayed until 6:30. Still nothing. I went home.

The next day, Edie was happy to see me. "Glad to see you made it."

Joanne smirked and winked at me.

"Are we ready for another great day?" I asked Joanne?

"Are you okay?" she asked.

"Yeah." The early morning traffic kept me busy. Ted came in for his usual, and I pulled him aside to find out what was happening.

"Susan is biding her time in case we're keeping an eye on her."

"Are you keeping an eye on her, that is?" He didn't have a chance to reply since Edie came over to talk to him. She reminded me to get back to work.

"What a bitch," I said to Joanne.

"Edie doesn't like her employees to be out sick," Joanne told me. Tough break. Thankfully, I didn't see Edie until the end of the day. My boss caught up with me and told me the coffee shop had no sick leave for their employees, so I would be docked for the days I was out.

This job may not work out.

On the way home, I checked my messages with my cell phone. Hall hadn't called.

I called him. "Nothing yet. What do you think then?"

"You think I'm going to tell you?" I was surprised at Hall's sarcasm. "Look, I have to go," he said.

"Is someone covering Lacey and Jess' house?" I hurried on.

"Do you think I would ever tell you," yelled Hall as he hung up. Oh, oh.

This was going too slow for me. Maybe I could do something to jazz it up. Food would help me think. There was a convenience store up ahead. I got a bag of peanuts to sustain me the rest of the way home. During the uneventful early evening, my mind kept returning to the Rod and Gun Club issue, and I decided I would go the following night. When nine o'clock came, Muffy and I were both in bed, content to let the rest of the world do their thing without us.

Edie was out the next day, and the girls that I worked with were more relaxed. Joanne and I joked about Edie finding a live one and running away with him. "Any guy with a pulse would do," I joked.

Ted came into the donut shop for his usual and pulled me aside. "Want to go out tonight?" he asked.

"Sure," I said, "What did you have in mind.?"

"My two favorite wrestlers are competing in Portland."

My smile turned sour. "No thanks, Ted. I think I'll pass. Besides, I've got plans."

"Oh?"

"Don't let your imagination go wild. I'm going to the Selectmen's meeting. The Rod and Gun Club are still trying to get their permanent liquor license."

"After all that's happened as a result of their last meeting, I shouldn't think you'd want to be anywhere near there tonight," said Ted.

Lines were forming at the register, and Joanne was trying to get my eye.

"I'm a glutton for punishment, Ted. I've got to get back to work. See you tomorrow."

The atmosphere in the donut shop was loose and free, yet I noticed we got our work done. Everyone knew what they must do, and we did it. Edie didn't have to bitch the way she did. I thought more and more about quitting. But what would I do?

When five o'clock came, I danced out the door. I was feeling good; the day had been productive, and all was right with the world.

At seven that night, after a delicious steak dinner at home, I chose a seat in the back of the Sandy Ridge High School auditorium., sitting on the right side. It felt good not to have to write feverishly and talk with people I didn't want to talk with. I saw a reporter I'd never seen before doing just that. He must be covering it for The Courier.

Olsen was his usual obnoxious self. Cheers and boos highlighted the meeting depending on the stance people took on the issue. It was hard to believe these men had responsible jobs in the community and were family men. They were acting like babies tonight, whining and wanting their way.

I stood up to leave. I was bored, and the matter didn't concern me anymore, I told myself. Moving up the aisle to one of the exits, a door on the opposite side opened, and Susan walked in.

I ducked into the shadow. Susan looked around. No one paid her much notice, thinking she was just another resident interested in the subject of the meeting.

Susan spied her father and moved down the aisle. I noticed there was an empty seat next to the man. Not for long, I thought. When Susan was making her way into the aisle, he saw her and started moving quickly out the other way. She caught up with him, dug her long fingernails into his shoulder, whispered something to him, and they proceeded out to the aisle, moving toward the exit.

Noiselessly, I made my way to the door they exited. Nobody even noticed what I was doing, so intent were they on bickering. I didn't go out the same door but chose the one closest to me. It made a sound, and I shrank back and waited a few minutes before trying to open it again.

My heart was in my mouth as I opened the door again slowly. I had no idea where Susan was. There was an overhead above me that shadowed me, and I took advantage of that. Soon, I heard them across the parking lot near the woods. Was this how it had happened with Blaire? Was history repeating itself? I trembled in the darkness.

"I don't know you. Please go away. I have a family now, and they don't know about you. I'm sorry about your pain, but you can't expect me to change my life because you came into it," he said.

Susan was torn between anger and pleading.

"You owe us, Lacey and me," she was saying, "You owe me for the years you weren't with me. I can tell Lacey still loves you. Come back to us."

The man in front of me turned. I pushed back against the building, hoping I couldn't be seen.

"This is crazy. I'm going back in. If you want money, come to my office tomorrow, and I'll give you some money."

Susan stared at him in disbelief. "Do you think this is about money? What kind of guy are you? I'm your daughter."

Oh, poor Susan. How demoralizing this was for her, pleading with someone to pay her attention, to acknowledge her.

"Who says?"

"Who says what?" she asked.

"Who says you're my daughter? Just like the other one. She said she was my daughter, too."

"The other one? Do you mean Blaire?"

The man came very close to Susan. He grabbed her shirt and shook her. Shit. Susan tried to push him, but he had hold of her, and she looked like a rag doll swinging her hands in vain. I wouldn't have thought to look at this guy he was that strong.

"Look, before you get hurt, you better leave."

"What happened to Blaire?" Susan asked. "Did you meet her? See her? When?"

He turned to leave and go back into the auditorium. Susan got a running start and jumped on him, but she was no match for him. He belted her, and she flew through the air like a falling leaf. I thought she must be unconscious, but madder than hell, Susan ran after him again, caught his legs, and he tripped.

He got up with a savage look on his face that made me cringe. I wanted to cry out to Susan when he started toward her, but I opened my mouth, and nothing would come.

"A spunky pair you are."

"Who?" Susan cried out.

"I didn't mean to kill her, you know. It was an accident. She wouldn't leave me alone, kept saying she'd go to my wife. She was going to the newspaper to expose me. I couldn't have that. Now, I have to do the same to you. Why did either one of you come here? She was going to tell my wife. I can't count on you to keep quiet." He shrugged. "They'll just be another accident, that's all."

"Police know it wasn't an accident. You pounded Blaire's head continuously." Susan was crying, "How can you say that was an accident? We never wanted anything from you except love." She was hysterical, fearful, yet scared.

I didn't know I was crying until I felt the drops land on my hand.

He came closer to her and grabbed her by the hair. Susan cried out in pain. My body shuddered as I saw him drag her to the woods.

I had no idea what I was doing, and I saw myself running towards them, shouting, "Stop! Stop, you can't do this," It was like an outer body experience. I saw myself, but I was observing someone else, someone I didn't know.

They both turned, surprised at my presence, and he lost his grip on Susan. She kicked him in the shins. The man didn't know what to do next. Should he pursue Susan, but what would he do with me?

I heard sirens and thought my ears were deceiving me. His face was in a panic.

"Give it up," I said, "That's the police," I had no idea that it was the police. It could have been an ambulance passing by. I prayed not.

He ran. He ran right into the face of the police car lights. Cops swarmed out like bees after their nest had been attacked.

Ted and Hall got out of the first police car and rushed over to me. "Are you alright?" Ted wanted to know.

"Where the hell did you come from?"

The men looked at each other and grinned.

"We were following you," said Hall,

"We knew you'd get into trouble if we gave you enough room," added Ted gleefully. "While you were in with Susan, we put a GPS on your car."

Smart ass.

Looking at Ted and Hall, I couldn't do anything but hug them. Then I remembered Susan. She was near the woods crying. I could feel her pain and did the only thing I could and hugged her.

"Come on, Susan. I'll take you home. It's over."

"Want a ride?" Hall asked.

My knees did feel shaky, "We'll take you up on that, I think. What do you say, Susan?"

She nodded. "We can pick up our cars later. Just don't ticket us," I told Hall.

Turning toward the cruisers, I saw the police cuff Burt Olsen and read him his Miranda Rights.

THE END

Made in the USA
Middletown, DE
28 May 2024

54942479R20183